BUCK

GEMS OF WOLFE ISLAND FOUR

WOLFES OF MANHATTAN TEN

HELEN HARDT

BUCK

GEMS OF WOLFE ISLAND FOUR

Wolfes of Manhattan Ten

Helen Hardt

This book is an original publication of Helen Hardt

Cover Design: The Killion Group, Inc.
Edited by Eric J. McConnell

Paperback ISBN: **978-1-952841-13-2**

PRINTED IN THE UNITED STATES OF AMERICA

For Mare.
Shunta.

ALSO BY HELEN HARDT

Follow Me Series:

Follow Me Darkly

Follow Me Under

Follow Me Always

Darkly

Wolfes of Manhattan

Rebel

Recluse

Runaway

Rake

Reckoning

Billionaire Island (Wolfes continuation)

Escape

Gems of Wolfe Island (Wolfes continuation)

Moonstone

Raven

Garnet

Buck

Steel Brothers Saga:

Trilogy One—Talon and Jade

Craving

Obsession

Possession

Trilogy Two—Jonah and Melanie

Melt

Burn

Surrender

Trilogy Three—Ryan and Ruby

Shattered

Twisted

Unraveled

Trilogy Four—Bryce and Marjorie

Breathless

Ravenous

Insatiable

Trilogy Five—Brad and Daphne

Fate

Legacy

Descent

Trilogy Six—Dale and Ashley

Awakened

Cherished

Freed

Trilogy Seven—Donny and Callie

Spark

Flame

Blaze

Trilogy Eight—Brock and Rory

Smolder

Flare

Scorch

Blood Bond Saga:

Unchained

Unhinged

Undaunted

Unmasked

Undefeated

Sex and the Season:

Lily and the Duke

Rose in Bloom

Lady Alexandra's Lover

Sophie's Voice

Temptation Saga:

Tempting Dusty

Teasing Annie

Taking Catie

Taming Angelina

Treasuring Amber

Trusting Sydney

Tantalizing Maria

Standalone Novels and Novellas

Reunited

Misadventures:

Misadventures of a Good Wife (with Meredith Wild)

Misadventures with a Rockstar

The Cougar Chronicles:

The Cowboy and the Cougar

Calendar Boy

Daughters of the Prairie:

The Outlaw's Angel

Lessons of the Heart

Song of the Raven

Collections:

Destination Desire

Her Two Lovers

Non-Fiction:

got style?

PRAISE FOR HELEN HARDT

WOLFES OF MANHATTAN

"It's hot, it's intense, and the plot starts off thick and had me completely spellbound from page one."

~The Sassy Nerd Blog

"Helen Hardt...is a master at her craft."

~K. Ogburn, Amazon

"Move over Steel brothers... Rock is *everything!*"

~Barbara Conklin-Jaros, Amazon

"Helen has done it again. She winds you up and weaves a web of intrigue."

~Vicki Smith, Amazon

FOLLOW ME SERIES

"Hardt spins erotic gold..."

~*Publishers Weekly*

“22 Best Erotic Novels to Read”
~*Marie Claire* Magazine

“Intensely erotic and wildly emotional...”
~*New York Times* **bestselling author Lisa Renee Jones**

“With an edgy, enigmatic hero and loads of sexual tension, Helen Hardt's fast-paced Follow Me Darkly had me turning pages late into the night!”
~*New York Times* **bestselling author J. Kenner**

“Christian, Gideon, and now...Braden Black.”
~**Books, Wine, and Besties**

“A tour de force where the reader will be pulled in as if they're being seduced by Braden Black, taken for a wild ride, and left wanting more.”
~*USA Today* **Bestselling Author Julie Morgan**

“Hot. Sexy. Intriguing. Page-Turner. Helen Hardt checks all the boxes with *Follow Me Darkly!*”
~**International Bestselling Author Victoria Blue**

STEEL BROTHERS SAGA

“*Craving* is the jaw-dropping book you *need* to read!”
~*New York Times* **bestselling author Lisa Renee Jones**

"Completely raw and addictive."
~#1 *New York Times* **bestselling author Meredith Wild**

"Talon has hit my top five list...up there next to Jamie Fraser and Gideon Cross."

~*USA Today* **bestselling author Angel Payne**

"Talon and Jade's instant chemistry heats up the pages..."

~RT Book Reviews

"Sorry Christian and Gideon, there's a new heartthrob for you to contend with. Meet Talon. Talon Steel."

~Booktopia

"Such a beautiful torment—the waiting, the anticipation, the relief that only comes briefly before more questions arise, and the wait begins again... Check. Mate. Ms. Hardt..."

~Bare Naked Words

"Made my heart stop in my chest. Helen has given us such a heartbreakingly beautiful series."

~Tina, Bookalicious Babes

BLOOD BOND SAGA

"An enthralling and rousing vampire tale that will leave readers waiting for the sequel."

~Kirkus Reviews

"Dangerous and sexy. A new favorite!"

~*New York Times* **bestselling author Alyssa Day**

"A dark, intoxicating tale."

~Library Journal

"Helen dives into the paranormal world of vampires and makes it her own."

~Tina, Bookalicious Babes

"Throw out everything you know about vampires—except for that blood thirst we all love and lust after in these stunning heroes—and expect to be swept up in a sensual story that twists and turns in so many wonderfully jaw-dropping ways."

~Angel Payne, *USA Today* bestselling author

WARNING

The Gems of Wolfe Island series contains adult language and scenes, including flashbacks of physical and sexual abuse. Please take note.

PROLOGUE

ASPEN

Katelyn sits, quiet, stroking Jed's soft head. Luke left an hour ago to fetch Edgar.

I can hardly look at my friend. My request put her fiancé in danger.

Another hour passes.

Then another.

Katelyn will never speak to me again if Luke doesn't come back.

Neither of us can sleep, neither of us can eat.

It's after midnight now, and—

The back door opens, and a barking Edgar runs toward me. He and Jed check each other out.

I heave a sigh of relief, as Katelyn launches herself into Luke's arms.

"What took you so long? I've been so worried."

"I'm sorry, baby. I didn't want to worry you, but I took advantage of the time I had to case the place."

"No one saw you today?"

"No, I was very careful. I parked two blocks away and

sneaked in the back. It was dark, and I made sure no one was around."

"Thank God," Katelyn nuzzles her head in Luke's shoulder.

I want to ask him what he found. I want to ask who might have done this to Buck.

But I stay quiet, let him and Katelyn have their time right now.

I take Edgar into the kitchen to get him some water. I find Jed's kibble and give Edgar a small portion. "Tomorrow I'll go to the store and get you some treats, okay?"

He ignores me as he guzzles down the food.

Luke comes in the kitchen to find me. "We need to talk, Aspen."

My stomach drops.

"No. Is it Buck? He's okay. Please tell me he's okay."

"Yes, Buck is okay. I got an update from my contact. He's sleeping soundly and his vitals are strong."

"Thank God." A sigh of relief whooshes out of me like a gust of wind.

"No, we need to talk about what I found at Gloria's house."

I nod. I'm exhausted, but I won't be able to sleep anyway. "Tell me."

He takes me to the family room, and I sit down on the couch. Katelyn sits next to me, and Luke sits on her other side, turning to face both of us.

"When I got to the house, the bodies—"

I wince.

"I mean Gloria and her husband... They weren't there."

I drop my jaw.

"Sometime between the time I got Buck out of there and

took him to the hospital and when I went back to pick up Edgar, someone moved the bodies."

"What does that mean?" Katelyn asks.

"It means someone took away the evidence. The place was clean. There was absolutely no evidence of blood anywhere."

"But there was so much blood on the bed, and some of it had seeped onto the carpet."

"Cleaners," Luke says. "Professional cleaners. They can get blood out of anything. There is absolutely no evidence that anyone died in that room or anywhere in the house."

"That's why you were gone so long," Katelyn said.

"Yes. I told you I wanted to case the place. Cleaners had been there, so I had to look even more thoroughly. See if I could find anything they might've missed."

"But you didn't find anything," I say.

"No, I didn't."

"But Edgar was still there."

"He was outside. Whoever had been there put him outside."

"But he was inside when you left with Buck, right?" I ask.

"Yes. He was. And I left him inside with a full bowl of water and a full bowl of food."

Luke goes up a notch in my mind then. He didn't rescue Edgar while he was there, but he did make sure he wouldn't starve for the next few days.

"What does it all mean?" Katelyn asks.

"It means were dealing with professionals. Someone with a lot of money and a lot of clout had Gloria and Brian taken care of."

"Who?" I ask. "Who would've done this?"

"I don't know. But I will find out. For you and for Buck. I owe him."

Katelyn is rigid next to me, and I know exactly what she's thinking.

She loves me, and she cares about Buck because I care about him. She cares about Buck because he helped her when they were both being held by the drug lord.

But her first loyalty is to her fiancé, to Luke.

She doesn't want him in danger.

And now...he's going to be in danger.

Because of me.

I don't know what to say. I could tell Luke to stay out of it. That once Buck is released from the hospital, we'll go back to Manhattan and forget all about this.

But I can't.

Someone tried to harm Buck. Someone killed Gloria and her husband.

And it's all because of me.

This is my fault.

I need Luke's help. I need Luke's help to put a stop to all of it.

"Katelyn..." I begin.

She turns to me, swallows back a sob. "No, Aspen. Don't go there."

"I'm sorry."

"What happened to you and what happened to me. None of it is our fault."

"I understand that. But I'll let this go. I'll let it go for you. For Luke. Buck and I can go back to Manhattan. I don't need to know who was behind this. All I really need is to get on with my life."

Katelyn gazes at me. She wants to take me up on my offer. I can tell, but she won't.

She won't because she meets her fiancé's gaze.

And his blue eyes—they tell a different story.

He will *not* let this go. His reasons are somewhat of a mystery to me, but they strengthen my resolve.

I harden. I harden into a freaking statue.

Buck could have been killed. Gloria and Brian *were* killed.

Whoever sealed my fate those years ago is still out there. I *will* track them down. Not only for me, but for the man I love.

Yes, the man I *love*.

The confession inside my mind doesn't surprise me.

It's there.

As if it's always been there and it always will be.

I love Buck Moreno.

So I'm in. I'm all in. I gather every ounce of courage, mettle, and strength I possess, and let the fierce determination surge through me like fire.

Hello, old friend.

Garnet is all in too.

1

BUCK

My head feels like someone is demolishing a building inside it, and my mind is pretty much pulp, but one thing is for certain. Waking up in a hospital bed is a hell of a lot better than waking up in the deserts of Afghanistan with an infected wound and a tired and aching body.

Hell, in Afghanistan, waking up at *all* was a boon.

Finding out where the hell I am? That would be a bigger boon. At this moment though? I'm happy just to have a comfortable bed.

My thoughts are incoherent.

I just want to know where Aspen is.

Nothing else matters.

Everything else is fuzzy, but I remember her. I know that I love her. And that I never told her.

Thank God I'm still here.

Thank God I can still tell her.

It won't be like Amira. I should've told her I loved her,

especially under the circumstances—in the middle of a battle zone when anything can happen...and it most likely will.

I should have told her. Instead, Amira died not knowing how I felt. Not knowing she was loved.

And now? If possible, I think I love Aspen even more.

Correction. I *know* I love Aspen more.

Aspen is my forever.

I click the button to call the nurse.

Then I try to remember everything else.

I was at Gloria Delgado's house. I sent Aspen to the car...

I searched the place, grabbed Edgar...

Nothing after that.

Except...

A face in front of mine for a moment.

Damn.

It was Lucifer Raven.

Luke Ashton.

How did he get there? How did he get into Gloria Delgado's house?

I could figure it out if my head weren't so achy and full of mush.

Finally, a nurse in green scrubs enters my room. "Yes? You called?"

"Yeah." My voice is hoarse. "I need to know..."

"What do you need to know, Mr. Moreno?"

I open my mouth to speak again, but the words come out in a garbled groan.

"Let me get you some water."

I nod.

The nurse leaves and a moment later returns with ice water and a straw. "Here you go." She holds it to my mouth. "Take a drink. It will help your dry throat."

I suck in some water through the straw and—

It's like a soothing balm coating my throat. I continue to drink until I've nearly drained the small pitcher of water she brought me.

She moves it away. "That's enough for now. I probably let you take more than you should. We don't know how your stomach will react."

"My stomach's fine." My voice is still gravelly, but at least it's easier to talk. "In fact, I'm starving."

"I'll check with your doctor to see if you can have some breakfast," the nurse says. "Is that all?"

Is it? I called for a reason...

I clear my throat, trying to dislodge the gravel. Big mistake. Hurts like hell.

"No." I wince from the scratchy pain. "When did I come in? Who brought me in? And I need to see someone. Her name is Aspen Davis."

"Let me look at your chart." The nurse sits down in front of the computer terminal at the head of my bed and taps the keys. "You were brought in by a man late yesterday afternoon. Doesn't look like they got his name."

"Was he blond?"

"I'm sorry. It doesn't say here."

"And what happened to me?"

"The head laceration was the most serious thing. You had lost quite a bit of blood, and your blood pressure was quite low when you were brought in. We got your head stitched up and gave you a small transfusion. You also have a mild concussion."

"And Aspen? Aspen Davis?"

"There's a note here that you were asking for someone named Aspen, yes. But we don't have a number for her."

"My phone." I reach over the side of my bed, grasping.

"You didn't have a phone on you when you were brought in."

"ID?"

"Yes, you had your wallet on you."

"Who would..." I shake my head.

"Does it hurt to talk?"

Is it *that* obvious? I nod.

"I'll tell you what. I'll try to find this Aspen Davis for you. Anything else?"

"Ashton. Luke Ashton. Katelyn Brooks. If you can find either one of them, you can find Aspen."

"Luke Ashton? You mean Lucifer Ashton?"

I clear my throat again. Damn. I've got to stop doing that. "Yes, Lucifer Ashton. The son, not the father."

"I'll do my best. Try to rest, and I'll check to see if you can have breakfast." She leaves the room briskly.

I close my eyes.

What the hell happened?

I knew I wasn't alone in Gloria's house. I checked everywhere, though. Or did I? Clearly my instinct was on point. Because someone...

Someone kept me from getting back to the car to Aspen.

Someone was in that house.

Someone who most likely killed Gloria and her husband.

Someone who clearly wanted me dead, or at least out of commission.

Someone whose next target might be—

Aspen.

2

ASPEN

My room—one of several guest quarters in Luke and Katelyn's beach house—is pure decadence. A king-size bed, Egyptian cotton sheets, a down comforter that is somehow cooling. A mattress that conforms to my body, and a pillow that is the perfect height for my neck. Even the color scheme works for me. It's light blue and green with blond oak wood. Soft but not girly.

I couldn't have asked for better accommodations.

I insisted on Edgar being in my room with me, and I was glad to have the company, but he kept me up most of the night. He would jump on the bed with me, snuggle for a little while, get down, pace around the room sniffing, bark a few times.

This continued throughout the night.

I understand, of course. This isn't his home, and we aren't his people.

God, his people...

Buck tried to keep me from seeing it, and now I can't *un*-see it.

After five years on that island, I should be used to seeing horror. But despite being poked, prodded, abused, raped...

I never saw death on the island.

Now I've seen it, and it's not anything I ever want to see again.

The sun's rays stream into my bedroom and cast a glow across my bed. Even though I'm still fatigued for lack of sleep, I rise. Edgar will have to go out, and I need to see Buck.

As soon as possible, I need to see Buck.

Luke promised to tell me if there were any changes, and he didn't wake me at all during the night, so I suppose that means Buck is fine.

Unless...Luke didn't want to wake me, which is totally possible. Katelyn would have told him I need my rest, and Luke would have relented because he'll do anything Katelyn asks. But surely he would have woken me if Buck...

No. I can't let my thoughts go there.

Buck is fine. Buck *has* to be fine.

Chills skitter over my body. I leave the bed and throw on the lush pink velour bathrobe that Katelyn gave me last night.

I open the door, and Edgar scampers toward the kitchen. I walk to the kitchen myself, open the sliding glass door, and let Edgar out into the large yard. Then I gasp.

No fence. No freaking fence!

"Edgar, come back!"

Edgar stops, does his business, and then returns to the porch.

Thank God. The backyard heads straight to the beach. Clearly Edgar is well-trained and responds to "come back."

"Sit," I tell Edgar.

He obeys.

"Lie down."

And down he goes.

A fully trained dog. Gloria and Brian were good owners. He must miss them.

"Good dog," I tell him, as I pet his soft head. "I know you miss your people. But you're safe here. You're safe here with me."

I love dogs, but I never saw myself with a small one like Edgar. I always imagined I'd have a golden retriever or a lab, but this little schnauzer has wriggled his way into my heart. He's mine now. I look around the deck. What time is it, anyway? I didn't bother to look when I woke. I'm surprised Luke and Katelyn aren't up yet.

But just as I have the thought—

Katelyn steps out onto the deck. She's wearing a light pink tank and drawstring shorts, and her blond hair is piled on top of her head in a messy bun. "You're up early."

"Couldn't sleep."

"I couldn't either. Luke never even came to bed."

I widen my eyes. "He didn't? Where is he?"

"He's been in his office all night, working on stuff."

"What stuff?"

"Research, mostly. Checking in with contacts."

"About what?"

"About *you*, Aspen. And Buck. About who could have done this to you two."

I shake my head and sigh. "Oh, Katelyn, I never wanted him to get involved in this. The two of you have been through enough."

"I'd say you're right, because you are, but it's more than that." Katelyn places her hand on my shoulder. "Two people are dead. And Buck… I hate to think what could've become of Buck if Luke hadn't gone back."

I nod, unable to bring words past the lump in my throat.

Thank God Buck is okay.

Thank God the man I love is okay.

I didn't even know I loved him until I faced losing him.

I have to tell him.

I have to tell him I love him. I can't take the risk—the risk he took with Amira—of something happening to him without knowing how I feel.

Katelyn reaches down to pet Edgar. "He's a good boy. He didn't run off."

"No, and I was scared shitless he might. He's obviously well-trained."

Katelyn nods. "Jed is great too. He never goes anywhere. We thought about putting up a fence, but we didn't want to obscure the view of the ocean. And Jed? Sometimes he goes all the way down to the beach, to the ocean, dips his paws in, but then he comes running back."

"Where did you get him? Is he Luke's dog?"

"He's both of ours. He was a stray that used to hang out behind The Glass House where Luke was a waiter. Luke would feed him scraps, and then, when Luke returned to LA and I had to come out here for my father, I brought Jed with me. I suppose it's silly, but I felt like he was my link to Luke."

"It's not silly at all. I get it. Where is Jed now?"

"Probably in the office with Luke. He hardly ever leaves Luke's side. Even though I'm the one who brought him out here, he seems to know that Luke is the one who fed him all those months back in Manhattan."

"Dogs are loyal creatures," I say.

"They are." She ruffles Edgar's ears again. "He's going to be grieving for a while. Missing his owners."

"I want to keep him," I say. "I feel like I need to keep him. But..."

Katelyn nods. "You're afraid he'll lead the enemies to you."

"Yes. Whoever murdered Gloria and Brian knows about Edgar. If he's chipped..."

"He probably *is* chipped, but it's not the kind of chip that can track his location. It's just a chip that has his ID on it."

I draw in a breath, let it out to try to relax. "Sure. Probably, anyway."

Katelyn sighs. "You're right to be concerned. The people we're dealing with could've easily put a tracking chip inside a dog."

"But he's just a dog. He can't take care of himself. I can't abandon him."

"I know exactly how you feel. That's how I felt about Jed." She smiles. "Do you want some coffee?"

"Yeah. Can I help you with anything?"

"Katina's already up making it."

"Who's Katina?"

"She's our housekeeper. She lives on the other side of the house."

"Oh. I guess I just..."

"Didn't realize we had a housekeeper?" She shrugs. "I know, it's weird for me too. She stays out of the way. Plus, the evening you guys came over for dinner was her night off."

"You certainly live in the lap of luxury here."

"It's all Luke's doing. But you know what? I'd live in a shack with him. That's how much he means to me, and that's how much I love him."

"I understand the feeling."

Katelyn's eyes widen. "Are you and Buck..."

"In love? *I* am. I don't know about Buck. But I do know one thing. I'm going to tell him as soon as I see him."

"Are you sure?"

"Are you kidding me? After everything we went through on that island, I wasn't sure I'd ever feel any kind of emotion again." I close my eyes for a moment and revel in the fact that I can feel anything at all. "But this is unmistakable. It hit me when I found out he was hurt. I knew that I loved him, and now I'm even more determined to find out who's behind this because whoever it is almost took Buck away from me."

"I understand what you mean. I fell hard for Luke just that way. It doesn't seem possible, does it?"

"It seems *im*possible in fact. But I can't deny what I'm feeling."

"Have you ever thought..."

"What?" I ask.

"It's just that... Aspen, you've been through so much. And now Buck is going to be okay. The two of you have a chance to be happy together. Is it really necessary to go searching for these ghosts?"

I harden inside. It's instant, as if some kind of cement has cured around my heart. "They're not ghosts. They're real evil people who killed Gloria and Brian."

"Gloria and Brian didn't deserve to die in such a horrible way," Katelyn says. "But what if they *weren't* innocent in all of this?"

Katelyn's not telling me anything I haven't wondered a thousand times myself.

"I suppose that's the problem," I say. "I *do* think Gloria knew more than she let on, but now we'll never know, will we? She's gone. But tell me, Katelyn. Who the hell would want to hurt a high school teacher and volleyball coach? A former volleyball player who never did anything to anyone?"

"That's what she told *you*," Katelyn says. "But does it really matter in the grand scheme of things? You've already been through so much. Buck has already been through so much. Shouldn't the two of you be allowed to have a shot at happiness?"

"I want that. I do. More than you even know. But I can't just leave the past in the past, because it's *not* in the past, Katelyn. It's here now. In the present. It killed Gloria and Brian, and it almost took Buck away from me."

Katelyn doesn't say anything. Simply bites on her lower lip.

I can read her like a book. She cares about me, and she cares about Buck. She has good reason to not want us going after the people who are ultimately responsible for my fate.

I see her point. I do.

But two people are dead because of me.

I'm not going to let anyone else die.

Buck and I will find whoever is responsible.

And they will pay.

3

BUCK

"We can't find a number for Aspen Davis," the nurse says. "We got a lot of numbers for people named Davis in Aspen, Colorado.

"She's from..." Damn, my head hurts. What's the name of her suburb again? "I don't know. Some suburb of Denver."

"Try her parents. Darnell and..." Damn. "Lisa. Lisa Jane Aspen Davis."

"You know her mother's middle and maiden name?"

"Yeah, and I'm not sure how the hell I do, but I do."

She sighs. "I'll see what I can do."

"If you could get me a smart phone..."

"I don't have that authority."

"Where's my wallet? You said it was on me when I was brought in."

The nurse goes to the chest of drawers on the other side of the room, opens the bottom drawer, and pulls out a plastic bag with the hospital logo on it. "Your personal items are in here."

The bag is bulky. My clothes and shoes are inside. "Could you find my wallet, please?"

"We're not supposed to go through a patient's personals."

"But I'm asking you to."

"Oh, all right." She digs through the bag, pulls out my jeans, my army boots, and then...my wallet. She hands it to me.

I open it, pull out a credit card, and give it to her. "Please. Get me a smart phone."

"Mr. Moreno, I'm—"

"Please."

She bites her lower lip and sighs. "I'll see what I can do."

"Thank—"

I gasp.

In the doorway stands Beauty herself.

Aspen. My Aspen.

"Buck! Thank God you're all right!"

"Aspen."

The nurse turns. "You're Aspen?"

"Yes. Thank you for taking care of Buck."

"Buck? His ID says Antonio Moreno."

"That's my real name," I choke out. "But people call me Buck."

"I'll give the two of you some time," the nurse says, leaving. "Do you want the door shut?"

I nod. "Please."

Aspen sits down on the edge of the bed. She strokes her finger over my cheek, and her touch... God, her touch...

"Are you okay?"

"I've been better. But I'm going to be just fine, especially now that you're here."

"I was so worried. Luke promised you were going to be okay, but until I saw you for myself, I just wasn't positive."

"So it was Luke then. He brought me here."

"Yeah. I didn't know where to go, Buck. You told me to leave if you didn't join me in the car within five minutes, but I actually waited fifteen minutes."

"Baby..." I groan.

"Hey, no admonishing me." Her beautiful features harden. "I'm okay. I'm here. No harm done. And it was the hardest thing I ever did to leave you there at that house."

"I'm glad you did."

"I didn't know what else to do. So I drove straight to Luke and Katelyn's house. They're the only people I know here, anyway, and I knew Luke could help you. In fact, he's the only one I know who could."

"Seems I owe him again."

I groan. I never wanted to be beholden to Lucifer Raven. Not after what he did to Emily.

But maybe he's the proof that people can truly change. Fuck. I'm still not sure I believe it.

But he's taking care of Aspen while I'm not able to. That will change soon. I'm getting the hell out of here today.

I open my mouth to tell Aspen when a gray-haired and gray-eyed woman in a white coat walks in.

"Mr. Moreno," she says, "I'm Dr. Bridges. I apologize for being a little late on my rounds today. I had an emergency this morning. How are you doing?"

"I feel like I've been hit in the head," I say dryly.

"Your vitals look terrific," she says. "Let me just check the stitches, and then I'm going to need you to answer a few questions for me."

Dr. Bridges looks closely at the wound on my hairline.

Then she shines her penlight into my eyes. I squint against the harsh brightness.

"Eyes look great. Open please."

I obey and she peers into my mouth.

"Airway is good. Your saturation is great at ninety-seven, and your blood pressure is back up to normal now that you've had a transfusion. How's the pain in your head?"

"I can live with it."

This pain is nothing compared to what I've endured in my lifetime.

"Good. I don't think there's any reason to prescribe anything for the pain. Eight hundred milligrams of ibuprofen should do the trick."

"Sounds good to me. I don't want any narcotics anyway."

I saw too many of my buddies get hooked on those damned things during our tours. I'm not going there.

"Is this your wife?" Dr. Bridges gestures to Aspen.

"Oh no." Aspen shakes her head. "I'm his..."

"Significant other," I say. "My girlfriend. Aspen Davis."

At the word girlfriend, Aspen breaks into a beautiful and dazzling smile.

Good.

She likes being called my girlfriend.

It seems like such a juvenile term, given what we've both been through.

But it works, and she seems happy.

"So am I going to get sprung today, Doc?" I ask.

"I want to keep an eye on you for another few hours. But if your vitals remain stable, I think we can let you go this afternoon."

"Not any sooner?"

"Hush," Aspen says. "Listen to your doctor."

"That's good advice," Dr. Bridges says. "I'll leave you two to visit."

She whisks away and closes the door behind her.

"Aspen..."

She covers my lips with her two fingers. "Don't try to talk. I have a few things I need to say to you. And they can't wait."

4

ASPEN

I love you.

The words flash through my mind, and I know I need to say them. It's part of the reason why I'm here. But what if he doesn't return them?

Will I be embarrassed? Will I wish I'd never spoken my mind? My truth?

"What is it?" Buck asks.

"I just need to say..."

"What?"

I rise then. Fear slices through me, but why? I know what *real* fear is. So does Buck.

Confessing my love and then not hearing it back?

Why should I fear such a silly little thing?

Because...

Because I don't want this to be over.

And if he doesn't return my feelings... If he's only in this because the Wolfes are paying him...

The end will be in sight.

I can't. Not right now. Not until we've determined who's

responsible for my abduction, for the murders of Gloria and Brian.

"It's nothing," I say. "It can wait. You need your rest."

"Aspen..."

I place my fingers on his lips once more. His lips that are still so soft even though they're dry. He needs some lip balm.

"I'm fine, baby," he says.

"I know, and I'm so thankful for that. I want you to rest. When you get out of here this afternoon, you'll come stay with me at Katelyn and Luke's house."

"Aspen, we have a suite at the Peninsula."

"You need to be taken care of. I'm going to take care of you."

"That's sweet, baby, but you can do that at the hotel."

"Katelyn won't hear of that, and you know I'm right."

He doesn't reply.

"Listen. I know you don't really want to be staying at Luke's house. But he's been up all night. He was still in his office when I came here. He's been working, trying to figure out who's responsible for my abduction. He wants to help, Buck, and he has contacts."

"I have just as many contacts. Through the Wolfes."

"I know that. But Luke has underground contacts."

"Are you kidding me? So do the Wolfes."

"Please. Let him help."

Buck doesn't reply, simply closes his eyes.

"Try to sleep. I'll be here when you wake up."

I'm not leaving this room.

Right now I'm feel like self-flagellating a bit. I can't believe I chickened out.

"I love you," I whisper as softly as I can.

His eyelids flutter a tiny bit, but his eyes do not open.

A tingle of fear shoots through me. Did he hear me? Or is he already asleep? Or maybe he's in that alpha stage between asleep and awake.

And maybe...

I grab his strong hand, the one that's not hooked up to IVs.

I hold it in my own. I'm a big girl and I have big hands, but Buck's hands... They dwarf mine. Engulf them.

They're big and beautiful, with long fingers and square nails.

Everything about Buck Moreno is beautiful.

He was carved by gods.

Even in a hospital gown, he looks delicious.

I lean toward him, brush my lips over his.

His eyelids flutter once more, and this time they open.

"Baby..."

I swallow down all my fears, and they're not even real because I've encountered true fear in my life.

Except maybe this fear *is* real. My life isn't in danger, but it's okay to be apprehensive when I'm about to trust someone else with my heart. This is real in its own way, and it's important.

I must tell him.

Right now, this man needs to know how I feel.

"Buck..."

"Yeah?"

"I have to say this to you. I can't hold it back. I... I love you."

A smile spreads across his face. "Do you?"

"Yes. I do. I do."

God, please don't make me regret this.

He squeezes my hand. "I love you too, Aspen. I think I fell for you the first time I saw you."

Happiness surges through me as my heart flutters. "At the railway station?"

"Yeah. I know it doesn't make any sense. Even then, though, I was struck by you. I knew I felt something. I just wasn't sure what it was."

"I can't believe it." Giddy. I'm totally giddy. "I can't believe you actually love me back. I can't believe this is even happening."

"Me neither, baby."

"It seems so unreal. How could either of us even have emotions after what we've been through?"

"Of course we have emotions. Emotions are what make us human. Emotion is how you know, even after having been through hell, that *you* are still here. You're still alive. You're still human. You're still *you*."

His words speak directly to my heart, and I understand. I understand.

"You're amazing, Buck. And I love you so much."

"I love you too. So much, Aspen."

"Okay. Now you need to rest. You've made me so happy."

"As happy as you've made me."

I hold his hand up to my mouth, brush my lips over the top of it.

When I look at him again, his eyes are closed.

I won't leave this room. Not until Buck is released this afternoon. I don't want to let him out of my sight ever again. I know that's not possible, but it is at least doable for the next several hours.

Luke is working, and Katelyn has joined him. Neither of

them owes me anything, but I'm so happy to have them in my corner.

I'm not sure what I did to deserve any of this.

Buck's love. Katelyn's friendship. Luke's…friendship, I guess.

Plus my mother and father, who I should probably call.

My father wants to help as well. He probably doesn't have the kind of contacts that Buck and Luke have, but I know he has some from his SEAL days.

To think—I had forgotten he was a Navy SEAL.

Funny how my memory is back now.

Even the parts of it that I don't want.

DIAMOND GAVE me Nike running shoes this time.

"Why?" I ask her

"I just do what I'm told, Garnet. But use them. Use them to the best of your ability."

I nod. The running shoes mean only one thing. Whoever is hunting me today is as athletic as I am—probably more so.

After all, whoever it is hasn't been through hell for the last couple years.

In truth though? I'm probably in the best shape of my life. Running from these freaks, using my brain and hiding when I can, has kept me in better shape than the most vigorous volleyball training.

Running shoes.

"I'll need socks," I say.

"Yes, they're inside the shoes."

Sure enough, balled in the toe of each shoe is an athletic ankle sock.

"Do I get anything else? Clothes?"

She shakes her head. "I'm afraid not. Just the shoes."

Whoever is going to catch me wants me to run. He wants me to run hard. Once he captures me, he doesn't want to be bothered with having to take off my clothes.

Great. Just great.

A few of the girls have learned to have a sense of humor about all of this.

I have not.

I envy them sometimes. Their laughter. I'm not sure I'll ever laugh again.

"Anything else you can tell me?" I ask Diamond.

"I wish I could, Garnet. They tell me very little."

"I can assume that whoever is going to hunt me wants a challenge," I say. "Otherwise no shoes."

She nods but says nothing.

"So my assumption is correct?"

"I've said all I can say."

"Fine. I understand."

"Garnet?" she says.

"Yes?"

"Run. Run hard and run fast. As fast as you fucking can."

I widen my eyes. Diamond doesn't normally use profanity, so she means what she says.

"I will," I reply.

I will anyway, but now?

I really will.

An anvil lodges in my gut. No. Not now. I can't have anything weighing me down.

I breathe in and out as slowly as I can, and though I succeed in dislodging the imaginary anvil, my heart flutters rapidly.

Adrenaline. A surge of adrenaline.

That's what I need, and my body never fails me.

Please, don't fail me now.

I shove my feet into the shoes quickly. I don't bother to look around and watch Diamond drive the Jeep away.

I head to the hunting ground, armed only with running shoes, my strong body, and my wits.

No one to set me up.

No one to back me up.

This is a tropical island. The weather is never cold here. The humidity is thick, and the green foliage is abundant.

I hide as best I can, but still they find me.

They always find me.

I've been here a while, so I know where to find the water sources. Food is another matter. Tropical fruit is scarce. The powers that be left only a few trees that actually produce edible fruit, and of course the hunters all know where they are.

They ambush us there, knowing we eventually have to make our way there or go into starvation mode, which conserves energy. On the hunt, we need energy.

I keep my stomach full as best I can. Some of the girls don't eat what they feed us in the dorm. I always eat everything I'm given, whether I'm hungry or not.

Because when I'm out on the hunt, no way will I go to one of the food sources unless I absolutely must.

Water is much more abundant.

It doesn't always taste the best, but I can at least stay hydrated without being ambushed. At least it's clean. They don't want us getting some disgusting parasite. A shitting and vomiting woman isn't worthy prey.

I've learned, since I've been here, to listen.

My ears are better than they've ever been. Same for my eyes. Sometimes they hunt us in the dark, and we must be able to adjust.

In a way, I've become nothing more than an animal—except I'm an animal who has to keep her body free of hair. Because of course, that's what the hunters like. Completely shaven armpits, legs, pubic hair.

Nothing to protect us from the elements, not that human hair could even do that.

My long brown hair is tied back in a braid.

I don't particularly like it because it makes me vulnerable. Something they can grab onto. But having it hanging down, whipping me in the face, making me hotter than hell as I run—that would be worse.

We all have long hair here on the island—because the men like it that way, of course, and there's nothing around to cut it with, anyway—and I swear to God, if I ever get the hell out of here, I will never wear long hair again.

As quietly as possible, I make it to the first water source. I hydrate as best I can, but then I jerk.

Something rustles.

I'm not alone here.

I'm never *alone here.*

5

BUCK

Naked.

Naked and vulnerable.

They always take our clothes, make us stand naked to shame us.

These aren't Afghan military. They aren't Taliban. They're a small group of insurgents that don't even exist as far as news outlets are concerned. No SEAL has ever been captured, and that will remain the party line.

I'm shackled at my wrists and hanging. Except I'm not hanging. My feet are flat on the ground. But I'm stretched just taut enough to accommodate my height with my arms raised.

Which means, if I dare to relax my body—to succumb to the sleep that I crave—my body will go slack, and my shoulders will be pulled out of their sockets.

I've been there before, and the pain is unbearable.

Yet I've borne it. More than once, but this time?

I'm not going down.

Absolutely not going down.

And it pisses my captors off. Wolf and Phoenix are nowhere to be found. They were with me when we were raided, but they're not in this cell.

I'm sure they're somewhere else, in the same situation I'm in. Or—God help them—worse.

"You're going to talk now, asshole."

I jerk. I didn't even hear the man come in.

He speaks with an accent, but his English is good.

I say nothing.

"What's your mission?"

"Moreno, Antonio." My name, rank, and serial number come out of my mouth in a hoarse robotic tone.

"Yeah, we have that already. What's your mission?"

I repeat myself.

"All right then. Things are going to get messy, Moreno."

What will it be this time? They may dump water on me, electrocute me.

Been there. Done that.

They can whip me. Cut me.

Been there. Done that.

I've even had a knife held against my balls.

I winced like hell, but thank God I was rescued in the nick of time.

They could go for my balls again. A man can live without his balls. I don't particularly want to, but which do I value more? My balls or my life?

Never thought I'd have to make that choice, but I'll take life.

The only thing he holds, though, is a broom.

Great. He came to sweep the damned place?

Whatever.

But when he slides the broom between my ass cheeks, I know what I'm in for.

I wince as fear lances through me.

Fight the fear. Fight the fear. Fight the fear.

It exists only to hinder you. To fuck with your mind.

Adrenaline. I fucking need adrenaline. But when you're hanging by your wrists and trying to keep your feet flat on the ground... When you're thirsty and hungry and so damned tired you can hardly keep your eyes open... Adrenaline is pretty hard to come by.

But when you're facing violation by a fucking broom handle?

Adrenaline surges.

Will I be able to keep quiet this time?

How badly will it hurt?

In another thirty seconds, I find out.

I JERK AWAKE. Where the hell am I?

Damn, the pain.

The bloodied violation, and the torturous, agonizing, humiliating pain.

I'm in a bed, but even now I feel it.

The tearing of my flesh, the blood trickling over my balls, my thighs, my calves...

"No!" I roar.

"Buck? Buck? Are you all right?"

A beautiful face hovers above me.

I face I recognize. A face I love.

"Aspen. Baby."

"You were screaming. You must've been having a dream."

"More like a nightmare."

"I should thank you," she says. "I was having a hellish nightmare myself, and your scream woke me up."

"I'm sorry."

"Please. Don't be. Are you okay? Do you want to talk about it?"

Do I want to talk about it? To the woman I love?

Hell, no.

I'm not the guy whose manhood is threatened by something he had no control over. Still, to admit what happened to me to the woman I love? Who's probably been through worse?

Not happening. At least not today.

"No, baby. I don't want to talk about it."

"What can I do for you then? Do you need some water?"

My throat is parched again. "Yeah. Water sounds great."

"I'll get some."

A moment later, she's back, holding water to my lips. I suck some through the straw and then let it go. "Thank you."

"It's been a few hours. Maybe we can get you out of here now."

"Dr. Bridges said this afternoon."

"I know, but I don't like seeing you in here, Buck. It... It scares me a little."

"I'm fine, baby. Nothing to be scared about."

In fact, my head feels better. Nothing like a few hours of sleep and a raging nightmare hurling me back to the worst time in my life to get rid of a headache, I guess.

Aspen takes a sip of the water she previously held at my mouth. "I want you out of here. I need you at home."

"At home?"

"Well...at Luke and Katelyn's home."

God. Staying at their house.

I don't know if I can do it.

But Lucifer Raven most likely has much better security at his home than I can get at the Peninsula Hotel.

I sigh. This means a great deal to Aspen, and I'll do anything for her.

And maybe... Maybe if I give a little, she'll give a little back. Maybe she'll ease up on this vengeance thing.

She needs to let this go.

She's going to end up in danger again, and damn...

What if I hadn't known someone else was in Gloria's house? What if Aspen had been there with me? And what if...

What if we *both* were hit in the head, left to bleed out?

We'd be dead now. Both of us.

I can thank my SEAL training for knowing we were not alone.

It wasn't a sound so much as a feeling.

And I was right.

I have to protect Aspen at all costs, and not just because the Wolfes are paying me to do it.

Because this woman is my life.

My whole life.

I *must* keep her safe.

And that includes keeping her safe from herself.

6

ASPEN

By evening, Buck and I are back at Katelyn's house.

Jed and Edgar are both happy to see Buck, which is odd, since neither of them really knows him. But dogs are like that. They're just happy creatures, as long as they're loved and fed.

Katelyn made up an additional guestroom for Buck, which makes sense. She doesn't know that we're in love now. Well, she knows I am, but she doesn't yet know that Buck returns my feelings.

"You're resting for a few days," I tell Buck once we get him situated in his room.

"I'll still be sneaking into your room tonight," he says.

"No, you will not. If anybody does any sneaking, it's going to be me. You're to stay in bed and rest."

"If you sneak into my room, Aspen, I won't be getting any rest."

"You let me take care of your rest. I will see that you get everything you need, including lots of sleep. I'm not letting you out of my sight."

He lets out a yawn. "Damn. All I've done is sleep for the last twenty-four hours and I'm still tired."

"Your body is still healing."

"I suppose. I'll be better tomorrow, and we can figure things out."

"Katelyn's going to bring you some dinner in a few minutes."

"For God's sake, this is ridiculous. I can join the rest of you for dinner."

"No. I'm putting my foot down." I smile.

"You're putting your foot down?"

I whip my hands to my hips. "Yep. Totally putting my foot down. You're going to get coddled and pampered and everything else I can do for you. At least until tomorrow."

"Tomorrow I'll be good as new."

"I will be the judge of that." I rise, give him a quick kiss on his forehead. "I'll be right back with your dinner when it's ready."

I close the door behind me and join Katelyn on the deck with the dogs. Luke is with her.

"Aspen..." Katelyn is frowning.

"What? What's going on?"

"I have some information from my sources," Luke says.

"And...?"

"And you remember Ice Man?"

I wrinkle my forehead. "Ice Man? I don't know what you're talking about."

Katelyn strokes Jed's head. "I suppose I didn't really tell you about him while we were on the island. God knows I'd rather forget about him now. It was one of the men. He took a liking to me. His specialty was humiliation."

My stomach clenches. "I won't ask you to elaborate."

"Good. I don't really want to. Suffice it to say, he's still at large. He was in Manhattan, and he came into The Glass House one time when I was there and Luke was waiting tables. He and Luke got into it on the street."

"Oh." A black feeling of doom crawls through me.

"He ended up figuring out who I was, as well," Luke says. "Somehow he got involved with King, and that's how I ended up back here in LA to take care of business."

"But he didn't get caught?" I raise my eyebrows.

"No," Luke says. "He didn't. We took King down, so we thought that would be enough. King and his close set of minions. I got to keep my immunity for the efforts, but Ice Man—Chris Pollack is his name—is still at large."

"I don't understand," I say. "If he was one of the men from the island, why isn't he in prison?"

"For the same reason I'm not," Luke says. "He turned on some cronies. Got himself an immunity deal."

"I guess I don't understand what all of this means."

"He held me at gunpoint," Luke says. "So we can get his immunity revoked based on my testimony."

"But you also falsely imprisoned him," Katelyn says. "We don't want to take a chance on *your* immunity."

"I'll be fine," Luke says. "My immunity deal, the current one, happened after I did that, so it will have no bearing."

"What does he have to do with this now?" I ask.

"He's been spotted here in town," Luke says. "Near Gloria Delgado's house."

I feel sick. Really, really sick. Like I could puke all over Katelyn and Luke.

"So you think maybe..."

"I don't know yet," Luke says. "But this isn't something we can ignore. This guy is a derelict. A psychopath. Clearly his immunity doesn't mean anything to him, or if it does, he can't help himself. Which makes him even scarier."

"Luke, he needs to be behind bars," Katelyn says.

"You'll get no argument from me. The man is a degenerate. Hell, I'd kill him myself if—"

"You will not," Katelyn says adamantly. "You will not do anything to risk what the two of us have right now."

"Katelyn, sweetie, the most important thing in my world is you. I have to protect you, and if that means—"

"No," Katelyn says again, this time whipping her hands to her hips. "I won't allow it. I simply won't allow it. Risking you is not worth it to me."

"But if this guy is at large," Luke says, "then *you* could be at risk. I will not risk *you*."

"Then I think we're deadlocked. Neither of us will risk each other."

Love passes between them. It's so thick it's almost visible.

I see it, and I feel it, because I understand it now. It's what I have with Buck. Funny, it's so much stronger and more passionate than what I ever felt for Brandon or anyone else.

"My father will help us," I say.

"He will?" Katelyn says.

"Yeah. He wants to. He's an ex-Navy SEAL like Buck. Only he was a high-ranking officer. He's six feet six inches, three hundred and fifty pounds, not an ounce of fat on him. He looks twenty years younger than he actually is."

"Aspen," Luke says, "do you really want to bring your family members into this?"

His words hit me in the gut.

"No. I guess I don't. But my dad—"

"I'm sure he was a hell of a military man, a hell of a SEAL. But he doesn't have the contacts that I have, and he doesn't have the contacts that the Wolfes have. It's probably better to leave him out of it. To ensure his safety."

Safety.

Safety is important to me. Especially now—now that I'm free again.

But what's also important to me is making the people who did this to me pay.

Finding them, getting my revenge.

Is it more important than my safety? Buck's safety?

My father's safety?

Buck's and my father's for sure.

But I'm willing to risk myself.

As fucked up as that sounds.

Which means...

Damn.

I'll have to do this without Buck.

Without Katelyn and Luke.

I'm going to have to go solo.

I hate the thought.

I hate the thought of leaving Buck.

But I can't risk his safety or my father's.

I can't risk Luke and Katelyn. They've already done too much for me, and they've found their happiness.

But you've found your happiness too, my inner voice says.

True. I'm in love. I'm so very much in love with Buck Moreno.

He's everything.

Everything I could ever want.

Which is why I must walk away.

I must walk away from Buck.

From my parents.

From Luke and Katelyn.

This is *my* journey. *My* path.

No one's but mine, and two people are already dead because of me. Gloria and Brian will never see the light of another day. I can't risk that happening to Buck or anyone else I love.

But if I walk away... I also walk away from Buck's contacts, from Luke's contacts.

Even my father's limited contacts.

Damn.

What to do?

"Aspen!"

I jerk toward Katelyn's voice.

"I called you three times. Where are you?"

"Just thinking." I force a smile.

And I do mean force. I don't *want* to leave Katelyn and Luke. I sure as hell don't want to leave Buck.

But Buck needs to heal.

Edgar scrambles at my feet, and I give him a pet. When I leave, I'll have to leave Edgar as well. This silly little ball of fur that makes me smile even when things are bleak.

But Katelyn will take care of him. He and Jed will form a pack. They've already become good friends.

Katelyn rises. "I'm going to check with Katina on dinner."

Yes, I have to eat. I have to make sure Buck eats.

I must keep up my strength.

I have twelve hundred dollars cash in my wallet. One credit card that gets billed to the Wolfes.

That's it. All I have. The Wolfes would never cut me off, but if I use their credit card, they'll be able to track me.

So I basically have twelve hundred dollars.

I know this makes no sense.

I know I'm better off staying with Buck, Luke, Katelyn.

But I can't drag them into this. They've all been through their own hell.

I rise as well. "I'm going to help Katina get a tray together for Buck."

Luke nods.

He's thinking about stuff. About that Chris Pollack guy, who's still out there.

Am I better off staying?

Of course.

But three people I care about, who are in this house at this very moment, are *not* better off.

Katina finishes setting food on Buck's tray.

"I'll take it into him," I say, forcing another smile.

I carry the tray out of the kitchen down the hallway to the guestroom where Buck is situated. I open the door, staying as quiet as I can, and find him asleep again. He needs to eat. I should wake him.

But I can't bring myself to disturb him. His head laceration is healing well, and he looks peaceful. So peaceful.

He deserves to be at peace.

I set the tray on the table near the window. I'll come back and check later to see if he's eaten.

I brush my lips over his forehead, and he stirs slightly. But he doesn't wake up, so I quietly close the door and leave him alone. I rejoin Luke and Katelyn on the deck, where I dutifully eat my meal.

After all, you eat when you're fed. Not only on the island, but here as well. It's the way you keep your strength.

And I will need all my strength.

7

BUCK

I lie in a pool of my own blood.

I can't put into words the humiliation that I feel. It's almost worse than the physical pain from the brutal abuse I just suffered.

I'm hungry. So damned hungry. When did I last eat? I'm not sure.

All they give me is bread and water.

Stale bread that's often moldy.

But at least they keep me hydrated. Here in the desert, it's a necessity, and clearly I'm worth more alive than dead to them.

They think they've broken me.

For a few scant moments, they're right.

But I will rise again.

I always do. I'm the spirited buck, and nothing can keep me down.

I think of Leif, who we call Phoenix. He got the name because he's so good at getting out of scrapes. Better than the rest of us. He's like the mythical phoenix who always rises from the ashes.

I wonder if he's already out of here.

If he can, he'll come for me. But if he can't? He'll get the fuck out of here. When things get tough, it's every man for himself.

We all understand that.

Honor, courage, and commitment.

It's what we learn as SEALs.

It is why I did not break—why I did not give away my secrets—even during the most brutal punishment I've ever received.

And it's what keeps me together now.

Humiliation threatens to overtake me.

But I control it.

I stay outside of myself. I do not focus inward.

I focus only on what I learned in training—how to control my emotions and my actions, regardless of circumstance.

The humiliation does not define me.

What someone else did to me does not define me.

My pain does not define me.

And I will not succumb.

My eyes flutter open, and I'm in yet another room I don't recognize.

A large room, and I'm in a large bed, with a mattress that perfectly supports my aching body.

Right.

I'm in Ashton's house. Raven's house.

I inhale, and the fragrance of roasted chicken and vegetables wafts toward me.

I sit up in bed, and then I spy a tray of food sitting on the table by the window.

My stomach growls.

I'm hungry. I will eat. I need to keep up my strength.

Where's Aspen?

This is Lucifer Raven's house. Surely he has some kind of intercom system. I look on the wall, but I don't see anything.

Surely there's a camera somewhere in here, hidden. He has top-notch security. Fucks with my privacy, but I get it.

I wave my hands. "Aspen. I'm awake."

Of course I don't know where the hidden camera is, and Aspen certainly doesn't have access to it anyway.

I get up, shuffle over to the table, wearing nothing but my boxer briefs. I take the dome off the plate. It's chicken fajitas, along with all the fixings. They smell good—especially the smoky aroma of roasted peppers. I load a tortilla with meat, onions, peppers, guacamole, and cheese, and I take a bite.

Yes, real food. The last meal I had was the mushy lunch at the hospital.

Also on the tray is a glass of ice water and a can of Coke.

I go for the water.

The food is still warm, which means it was placed here recently.

What time is it? I have no idea. I don't know where my phone is—somehow it didn't make it to the hospital with me and Nurse what's her name never got me a new one.

When I finish my dinner, I go into the attached bathroom, take care of things, and then walk to the closet. Perhaps there's something I can wear.

Yes, a fluffy white robe—the kind you find in posh hotel rooms—hangs inside. Since it's all I have at the moment, I don it and then leave the bedroom.

An older woman in jeans and an apron stands at the counter.

"Mr. Moreno?"

"Yeah, that's me."

"You shouldn't be up."

"I'm fine. Are you the person I should thank for the delicious fajitas?"

"Yes, I'm glad you enjoyed them. I'm Katina, Mr. Ashton's housekeeper."

"Well, thank you again." I glance outside. "I guess I'll join the others on the deck."

"I should get you back to bed."

"Don't be silly. I'm fine." I smile, even though it makes my face ache. "And thank you again for the dinner."

"You're most welcome. Please let me know if you need anything else."

"Maybe just some more water?"

"Of course. But can I convince you to go back to bed first?"

"I'm afraid not."

"Very well then. I'll bring your water out to the deck."

"Thank you."

I step through the door to be met by Edgar and Jed.

"Buck!" Aspen stands. "What are you doing up?"

"I just ate the dinner you left for me."

"Good. I hope you swallowed every bit."

"I did. I was actually pretty hungry. I'm feeling better."

"That's good." This from Luke. "Because you and I need to talk."

"O...kay," I reply.

"Alone."

"Oh, hell no," Aspen says. "If you're going to talk about what's going on with me, I need to be involved."

"Actually, it's not about you." Luke's tone darkens. "It's about...my previous life."

Aspen doesn't look convinced, but she backs off.

"Now?" I ask.

"Yeah. While you're awake would be good."

I resist an eye roll. "Okay."

I follow Luke back inside the house, down the hallway on the other side of the bedrooms to what appears to be his office.

"Come on in." He takes a seat behind a large mahogany desk and gestures for me to sit down in one of the chairs on the opposite side.

When I drop into the chair, it's the most comfortable damned cushion my ass has ever sat in.

Or maybe I'm just that tired.

"What is it?" My tone is not friendly.

"I know you'll never like me. I've accepted that."

"Good."

Luke inhales and pushes some papers around his desk. "But we're on the same side here. We both want what's best for Katelyn and Aspen."

"Keep talking."

"Aspen has decided she doesn't want her father involved."

"Oh?"

"Yeah, and for what it's worth, I agree with her. You and I both have much better contacts than Darnell Davis. I looked into him. He was an excellent SEAL, highly decorated. He retired as a captain."

"I know all that."

"A man of integrity."

"All SEALs are," I say through clenched teeth.

"Which is why we need to keep him out of this. You and I both know that we're going to need to bend the law here."

I don't reply. He's right, but it still rubs me the wrong way. I don't like his implication that Darnell is a man of integrity but I am not. I *am* a fucking man of integrity, damn it.

Still, I'll break at every law on the planet if it means keeping Aspen safe. Does that affect my integrity? I don't feel like it does, but if so?

So fucking be it.

I feel like a snake is slithering up my spine.

"You haven't been able to talk her out of this?" I say.

"Was I supposed to?"

"She's hell-bent on vengeance, Raven."

"It's Luke."

I don't resist it this time. I roll my eyes. "Whatever. Luke."

"You've got to give me an inch, Buck."

"I don't have to give you a goddamned thing."

Luke sighs. "I understand."

And I think he does understand. The expression on his face isn't angry. It's resigned. Were our situations reversed, he'd feel the same way I do.

"But like it or not," he continues, "we're in this together. I love Katelyn and you..."

I clear my throat. Damn. Still hurts. "I love her. I love Aspen."

"I figured as much."

"Which is why I need to save her from this. From this fate. I know what it's like to want revenge so badly that you can actually feel your blood boiling. It almost broke me once. I won't let that happen to the woman I love."

"That's not your choice to make."

"I have to do what I can. And as much as I hate myself for it, I need to ask for your help."

"Part of me agrees with you," Luke says. "But part of me needs to see all these people taken care of. As long as any of them are still out there, both Aspen and Katelyn are in danger. I can't have that."

"I don't want that either," I say truthfully. "But I can't stand by and watch Aspen destroy herself for this cause that may never be put to bed."

"Oh, it *will* be put to bed."

"How can you say that?"

The look on Raven's face is no longer resigned. His cheeks have pinked, and his eyes are on fire. "Because I'll make *sure* it is. I'll make sure every person involved with taking any of those women—with anything that happened to them on the island—is either dead or behind bars for life."

"Do you still have your underground contacts?" I ask.

"One or two, but they aren't particularly forthcoming right now."

"Because you went canary."

"Yeah, and I'd do it again. I'd do it again because I would do anything for Katelyn."

"Even sacrifice your integrity?" I ask, my voice dripping with sarcasm.

"What is integrity anyway?" Raven scoffs. "It's doing the right thing when no one else is looking. I did that. Sure, I ratted out King and his minions. I did it twice. But it was the right thing to do."

I sigh. "I'd like to be able to disagree with you."

"But you can't."

I shake my head. "I can't. But betraying people who trusted you..."

"Really *bad* people," he says.

"I get that. I totally get that."

How I want to hate this guy.

But we're on the same fucking side here, and he has sources that I don't. And I'm beginning to see that integrity can be a little subjective.

"All right. Let's cut a deal then. We take care of everyone who had anything to do with Katelyn or Aspen or any of these other women being taken." I grip the arms of the comfy chair I'm sitting in. "But you have to do something for me."

"And what's that?"

"Keep Aspen out of it. She needs to let this go. It's too emotional for her."

"And it's not for you?"

"Of course it is. It's *damned* emotional for me. I love that woman. I'd like to personally execute every single person who's harmed her. And I mean *every single one*. Part of being a SEAL is learning to keep your emotions at bay. It's damned difficult sometimes, Luke, but I do it. And it's my personal belief that it's better for Aspen to just let this go."

He smiles. "You called me Luke."

I raise my eyebrows. "Seriously? That's what you got out of my monologue?"

"I figure it may be significant." Then his smile fades. "You say you want to keep your emotions at bay, that it's what a good SEAL would do. Yet you admit this is emotional for you, Buck, and it clearly is. It's written all over your face."

I grip the arms of the chair harder, steel myself, but emotion still pours out of me. "Seems I've found my Achilles' heel. And her name is Aspen Davis."

8

ASPEN

Katelyn and I play with the dogs a bit before going back in the house. Luke and Buck have been in his office for over an hour, and I'm so curious.

Curious what they're talking about.

How do I let them off the hook for this?

How do I make sure the three of them stay safe?

There's only one way.

"Katelyn?"

"Yeah?"

"What if I told you I'd let all of this go."

"You will?"

"I've kind of allowed this to overtake me. And now, because of my interference, two people are dead."

"Yes, I'm sorry for that." Katelyn pats my thigh. "It must be so difficult for you, and Gloria didn't deserve to die. Plus, she may have known more."

"I think Gloria *did* know more. I think that's why she's dead. I think that's also why her husband, who's totally innocent in all of this, is also dead."

"Still, you can't know for sure. This could've had nothing to do with you."

I shake my head. "That would be a little too convenient."

"Maybe. Is it too much to hope that it's all over?"

"It's not all over. Not for either of us, Katelyn. Not as long as Ice Man is out there."

Katelyn goes white.

"I'm sorry."

"It's okay," she says. "I know I'm perfectly safe here. I mean, this place is like a bunker. You wouldn't believe the security we've got."

"How much security *do* you have?" I glance around, scanning the area. "I mean, are you watching me get undressed tonight?"

"Of course not. But the guestroom cameras are turned on when no one's here."

"So every part of this house is covered?" I hold back a wince. How am I going to leave undetected?

"Every part," Katelyn says.

"You're not..."

"What?"

"It's just that... Buck told me about his sister. About how Luke kept her trapped inside the house."

This very house. I don't mention that fact.

"I know all of that," Katelyn says. "Luke and I don't have any secrets."

"Then you know that it was *this* house."

"I do. Luke offered to sell it for me. He said we could get our own place. But this place has been in his family for three generations, and I couldn't let him do that."

"So you don't feel any ghosts here?"

"I truly don't. Luke is not the same person that he was. I

never really believed people could change, but he's proof of it."

"What if Ice Man could change? Would you want him exonerated?"

Katelyn's lips tremble.

Good. I've made her think. Not that I don't want her to be happy with Luke. I do. I actually *do* think Luke has changed, and even Buck will admit it when I press him. Alcohol was a big part of Luke's problem. And for the rest of what was going on in his mind, he's been through therapy. He's probably still going.

But what about Ice Man? Or Chris Pollack, as Luke says his name is.

He wasn't a hunter, so I never had any run-ins with him.

But he was the one Katelyn hated the most.

Which is interesting because he didn't ever put a mark on her.

But it was the humiliation. The degradation.

I was humiliated on the island as well, but in a completely different way. Sometimes the scars you can't see are worse than the ones you can.

Just one more reason why I need to let Katelyn out of this.

I want her to be safe. Safe with the man she loves.

And now...

I'm so in love with Buck. And because I love him so much, I must leave. I must leave and do this on my own.

Everyone I love needs to stay out of it. My father. Katelyn. Luke. And especially Buck.

I don't know exactly what he went through during his tours, but I know it was as bad as or worse than what I went through on the island.

The best thing I can do for Buck—the man I love—is to leave him in peace.

9

BUCK

"I've got a lead on one of the men from the island," Luke says. "His name is Chris Pollack, and he was one of Katelyn's tormentors."

"And he's not in fucking prison?"

"No. Although by the time I get done with him, he will be."

I clench my fists. "He cut a deal then."

"So it would seem."

"I've seen the documentation," I say. "Most of the men who paid to hunt on Derek Wolfe's island have disappeared."

"Yep. Because they have the money to do so. We'll never find them. And frankly? It's probably best that we don't."

"How can you say that?"

"I'm just being realistic, Buck. These people have more money and power than the two of us can imagine, and if we stir up trouble with them, they'll hit us where it hurts."

I clear my throat. "Aspen and Katelyn."

"Bingo."

"But this guy, this Pollack. He's still around?"

"Yeah. I came into contact with him when we were in Manhattan. He came into the restaurant where I worked, and he recognized Katelyn. And like the moron he is, he approached her."

"Fucker. He's obsessed."

"That's right. He went so far as to find out who I truly am and make a deal with King. Didn't work out so well for him—King, that is. But Pollack is still at large."

"Do you think this is somehow related to what happened to Aspen?"

"There's no way to know. But as long as Pollack is out there..."

I clear my throat. "You want my help with Pollack, and you'll give me your help figuring out the Aspen situation."

"It's not a dealbreaker, Buck. That's not who I am. Not anymore. But yeah, I'd appreciate your help with Pollack."

I owe this man nothing.

Not a damned thing.

Yeah, it'd be nice if that were actually true, but if he hadn't rescued me from Gloria Delgado's house, I might have bled out on her freaking living room floor.

Plus, he does seem to love Katelyn, and he seems to genuinely care about Aspen.

"And if I say no?"

"If you say no, then your answer is no. I told you it's not a dealbreaker. I'm going to help you. I owe you. For Katelyn."

And I owe him, damn it. Fuck it. I've been to hell and back so many times. What's one more time?

These people have to be brought to justice.

"What kind of immunity deal did Pollack get?"

"The books are sealed. I've used all my sources to try to find out. Maybe the Wolfes have sources I don't."

"I suppose I could ask."

"I'd appreciate it."

"But whether or not we can find out the conditions of his deal, you want him eliminated."

"Not by my hand or yours. My days of participating in murder are over."

"Yeah, so are mine."

I lost count of the bodies that died by my hand in Afghanistan. After a while, they ceased to be human.

And that's the scariest part of all.

I clear my throat. "All right. I'll help you with Pollack. But Aspen has to take priority."

"As long as Katelyn stays safe and Pollack stays out of the picture, I'll make Aspen the priority. But if Katelyn is ever in danger..."

I nod. "Got it."

I'm starting to understand Luke better. He never loved my sister. No, he was obsessed with her, and the obsession was aggravated by his alcoholism and precarious mental health. He's sober now, and he's in counseling, according to Katelyn.

He loves her. He'll do anything to protect her.

And *that* I can get behind.

That I understand.

A yawn splits my face.

"You okay?" Luke asks.

"Yeah. Just tired and I've got a headache coming on. I need to take some more ibuprofen."

"What did the doc say? When can you get back to normal business?"

"As soon as I'm feeling up to it. Which means tomorrow."

"Good. Tomorrow we'll begin our search."

I rise. “Actually, the first thing I need to do is get some damned clothes.”

“Already done. Clothing will be delivered tomorrow.”

“I have money.”

“I know that. You can pay me back if it’ll make you feel better. Aspen knew your sizes, and she knows what you like. Army boots, jeans, button-downs. T-shirts and underwear. Some running shoes, swimwear.”

“All right. Just bill me.”

“Not a problem.”

“And Raven?” Shit. “Sorry. Luke?”

“What?”

“Thank you.”

“Don’t mention it.”

I nod. He doesn’t have to worry about that. This is the last time I’ll ever mention it.

10

ASPEN

Luke returns to the deck after a couple hours, and I'm ready to go to bed.

"Where's Buck?" I ask him.

"He was exhausted. He went to sleep."

A yawn creeps up on me. I was thinking about feigning one, but I didn't have to. "I guess I'll hit the sack as well. Thank you both for everything."

"Aspen," Luke says, "Buck needs his rest."

"Did I say I was going to disturb him?"

Katelyn smiles. "His best medicine might be Aspen."

"You're probably right." Luke sits down next to Katelyn.

Katelyn stares lovingly at the engagement ring on her left hand. "I hope one day you're as happy as Luke and I are."

"I hope so too."

But inside I know I won't be. I have to leave. Not just for Buck's own good but for Luke's and Katelyn's as well. For my father's.

This is something I have to do myself.

You're not thinking straight.

From my inner voice.

But perhaps I'm thinking straight for the first time in my life. Perhaps I just want to protect the people I love.

Is that so wrong?

I bring Edgar with me into the house and then to my guestroom. I take a quick shower and attempt to put on the pajamas Katelyn gave me. They're way too small. I'll sleep in the nude, I guess.

I'm determined to leave Buck alone.

Until I'm not.

I rise from bed, put on the fuzzy pink robe.

I love this man, and if I'm going to leave him tomorrow, I'm going to at least have this night with him.

I'll do all the work. He doesn't have to do anything.

No response to my knock, so I crack the door open.

Buck is asleep—or he seems to be—but then he opens his eyes.

"Hey, baby. I was hoping you would join me."

"Lie down," I say. "You need your rest."

"I'm never too tired to make love with you."

"Doesn't matter. You're not going to do anything. I'm going to do all the work, and I'm going to make this a night neither of us will ever forget."

He smiles, and then he groans. "Sounds perfect."

I shed my robe, letting it fall over my shoulders and onto the floor.

Buck sucks in a breath at my naked body.

My naked body with all its scars, its missing part.

Still, he loves me.

And I love him. So fucking much.

I walk toward him. Remove his covers, crawl on top of him.

I massage his thighs first, and then his dick, which is already hard.

I bite the tip of it through his boxers.

Then I slowly, languidly, move them over his hips.

His huge cock springs out.

Still I'm amazed at how I find this part of him so beautiful. There was a time when I wasn't sure I could ever bear to look at that part of a man again.

I take his cock, hold it at the base, and put the head between my lips. I moisten the tip with my saliva and then use it as a lubricant to move my fist up and down the shaft.

Then I go down. Force my mouth upon him, until I feel the tip at the back of my throat.

And I want this. I want it more than I ever thought I could.

I spread his legs and position myself between them, letting my breasts dangle. And I take him between my lips once more.

"God, baby," he groans.

I remove my mouth from him, take over with my hands. "Does it feel good?"

"God, you have no idea."

I swirl my tongue around his head, lick him from his balls to his tip. Then I use my fist again, both hands this time from shaft to head. I tongue him once more. Go down on him all the way to the base.

He tastes like sweat and man.

He tastes like Buck.

"Baby. Slow down."

But he's not in charge here. I am.

Part of me wants to cuff him, bind him to the bed, have my way with him. But Buck is a military man. He would never submit that way.

In fact, a big part of me would never want him to. Still, the idea is a bit of a turn on.

I continue blowing him, using my hand to increase the friction.

"Fuck," he says. "I need you. Need you on top of me."

"We'll get to that," I promise.

Then I return to my work.

"Baby, please..."

Part of me wants him to come in my mouth.

But do I want that more than I want to be on top of him right now? His cock deeply embedded inside me?

I don't think so.

I climb on top of him and sink myself down on his erection.

I move slowly, more of a back-and-forth movement than an up-and-down.

It hits me just at the right place, and I moan.

"That's it, baby. Make it feel good, Aspen."

He cups my breasts, thumbs my nipple and my areola where the other should be. Again, the phantom nipple emerges, and I feel it.

I feel it harden along with the other one.

"God, you're beautiful," he says.

And I hear the truth in his words. He doesn't care about a missing nipple. He doesn't care about scars.

I gaze down at his chest, run my fingers over all his scars as I continue to rock back and forth on top of him.

He winces slightly.

I gasp. "Did I hurt you?"

"No. God, no. You feel amazing. It's just... The scars..."

I lean down then, trail my lips over one scar. "It's you, Buck. It's all you, and it's all beautiful. You don't mind my scars, do you?"

"Of course not."

I raise my head. "Then why should I mind yours? Every mark on your magnificent body has helped make you who you are. It's the same for me. They all hurt, but they all made me stronger."

"My God," he says, reaching forward to cup my cheek. "How can you be so perfect?"

"Same way you can." I sigh and rock back and forth again.

"Touch yourself," he says. "Please."

I moisten my fingers in my mouth and trail them down to my clit.

His gaze drops to where we're joined. "You're so beautiful."

And in his eyes, I am. Just like in my eyes, he is.

So freaking perfect. Perfectly formed and perfectly beautiful, and his scars make him more so.

I circle my finger around my clit slowly, still rocking back-and-forth, letting every inch of his cock touch inside every inch of my pussy.

I gradually increase the movements of my fingers, until—

"Oh!"

The climax surges through me, and I'm no longer satisfied to rock slowly back-and-forth.

I piston my hips, screwing him harder and faster, until his strong hands grip my hips, pulling me above him.

"Buck?"

"Sorry, baby. I don't want to come yet. Not until I taste your sweet pussy."

"No. No work for you."

"All right. You don't want me to work? Then sit on my face. Sit on my face and rub that delicious cunt all over me."

I smile.

That, I can do.

11

BUCK

God, her perfect pussy.

Her fragrance is lusciously musky, her taste even better. I clamp my hands over her ass cheeks and I dive between her folds.

My God, I could eat her forever.

I kiss her. Kiss her pussy.

And then slide my tongue over her clit.

I squeeze the cheeks of her ass, massage them, and then spread them so her pussy is even more bared to me.

With one hand, I trail my fingers over her taut and muscular thighs, massaging her as I go.

All the while, I'm sucking her, and she grinds against my face, making me even harder.

Her mouth is back on my dick, I'm about ready to explode. Still, she's going slowly, as if she knows I want to give this to her now.

Her texture is like silk under my tongue. Sweet and tangy silk.

She moves her hips more now, grinding into me, moving her clit against my tongue, against my lips.

My God.

I could eat her forever and never tire of her fragrance, her flavor, her texture.

As she rubs against me, the need to penetrate her becomes unbearable. But I don't want to give up licking her. So one finger goes into her pussy, as I continue sliding my tongue between her folds and focusing on her clit.

She gasps, and then moves faster against my face.

God, she's so hot.

She's sucking the head of my dick softly. Just softly enough to keep me from coming. And I want more of her. Her sweet ass is right there. So tight and so available.

I doubt she's ready for that.

One day, though. One day when she's healed and ready.

She moans above me, grinds against me, and just when I'm about ready to explode, she flips her ass upward, crawls forward, and sinks down on my cock.

She's in reverse cowgirl position, and I have a bird's eye view of her beautiful ass.

She fucks me. And this time it's not soft rocking back-and-forth.

This time it's hard. This time it's fast. This time it's—

"Buck, my God!

She comes over me, and that's my cue.

I groan as the contractions start at my balls and move outward.

Everything, everything is Aspen.

Aspen, enveloping me, letting me come inside her.

Aspen, my love.

My only fucking love.

We climax together, and I'm not sure where my body ends and hers begins.

I realize then.

This is how it's supposed to be between lovers.

We are one now.

We can never be complete without the other.

THE SUN STREAMS into the bedroom.

I wake, and there's no more pounding in my head. I feel strong. Strong and fit and ready to face the world.

As long as my woman is at my side.

I turn to touch her, just to feel her nearness—

Then I jerk upward.

She's gone.

It's early yet. Not even seven o'clock according to the clock on the bedstand. But I don't hear the shower. In fact, the bathroom door is open.

Oh, of course. She went back to her own room to go to the bathroom.

That's where I'll find her.

She's probably in the shower right now, so I decide to surprise her.

Since we're in someone else's house, I grab the fluffy robe. Luke said my clothes would be here sometime this morning.

Doesn't matter. I don't need clothes for what I'm about to do.

I slide the robe over my shoulders and then leave my room. I'm steady on my feet, and I feel ninety-nine percent like myself.

Good. I need to be at full capacity. Not just for joining

Aspen in the shower, but for everything else that Luke and I must do.

The door to Aspen's bedroom is cracked. That's a little bit strange, but she knows neither Luke nor Katelyn would barge in.

I walk in, but I don't hear the shower running.

She must already be out. Too bad for me. But I can still catch her naked.

I head toward the bathroom.

12

ASPEN

I did my best to avoid Luke's security this morning. Last night, after I left the deck and before I joined Buck in his bedroom, I scoped the area from my room to the front door. I found several cameras and figured out how to avoid them. It was simple dumb luck that a siren didn't wail when I left. Thank God. I was worried that an alarm might be tripped.

My Uber driver drops me off at a rental car place.

I hated leaving Edgar, but I know Katelyn will take care of him. I'll be back for him, God willing.

If I come back at all.

Leaving Buck was the hardest thing I've ever done.

And yes, I know what that means. It means it was more difficult than every day I endured on that island.

And it was.

It gutted me.

Completely gutted me.

I almost couldn't do it.

The only reason I could? My undying love for him.

He deserves a life of peace. Especially after all he's been through.

He doesn't need to get mixed up in my life. And once I'm done? If I live to tell the tale? I'll go back to him.

And I hope like hell he doesn't hate me for what I'm doing.

13

BUCK

I run out to the kitchen. “She’s gone! Aspen is gone!”

Katina stands by the cooktop. “Yes, Mr. Moreno. Mr. Ashton is already on it.”

My heart is racing, but I force myself to draw in a calming breath. “Right. All of his security.”

Luke walks in then. “I’ve got a tail on her. An Uber driver picked her up, and then he drove her to a rental car place. She’s there now.”

“Let’s go get her.”

“I was just coming to wake you. I figured you’d want to go with me.”

“Of course. We’d better hurry though. And I don’t have any clothes.”

“Your clothes were just delivered.”

My mind races. “What if she leaves the rental car place?”

“She won’t. I’ve got people in place to keep her there until we arrive.”

I open my mouth.

Thank you. The words want to come out, but I can't get them to move.

Luke doesn't seem to mind though.

"The packages containing your clothes are right by the front door. Get dressed, and we'll leave as soon as you're ready."

I nod.

Damn. Aspen. What the hell was she thinking?

I grab all the boxes and take them to my room. Two pairs of shoes—army boots and a pair of running shoes.

I choose the running shoes. If Aspen's going to run from me, I'm damned well going to catch her.

I pull on a pair of jeans and a T-shirt. Then the runners.

That's all I need here in LA.

I haven't showered, and I'm a mess, but I don't care. Getting to Aspen is more important.

I walk out of my room and back to the kitchen. "I'm ready," I tell Luke.

"All right. Let's go."

"What about Katelyn?"

"She's out on the deck with the dogs. She knows what we're doing."

"Wait. Dogs? As in plural? She left Edgar here?"

"I know. Strange. But it makes me think..."

"Yeah, me too. And I don't like it."

If she left Edgar here, she knew she wasn't going anyplace where she could take care of a dog. She trusted that Katelyn would take care of him, which she will.

God. Why, Aspen? Why do you keep running?

This is the third time.

Well, to be fair, it's only the second time.

The first time was when she left Manhattan without

telling anyone. The second time, she just went down for a workout. She just didn't bother telling me.

So I guess this is really the second time.

Why would she leave me? She said she loves me.

I follow Luke out to his garage, and we get in his Tesla.

He turns to me, and it's as if he read my mind. "She's afraid. She's afraid she can't control herself—this desire she has for revenge. And she loves you too much to keep you involved."

"That doesn't make any sense," I say, even though in my heart I know it does.

"It does, actually. What if you had the chance to get revenge on the people who have harmed you? And you knew it would put you in danger? Would you want her involved?"

Damn it. I hate that I'm beginning to like this guy. He's making sense. A lot of fucking sense.

"Of course not. I'd protect her at all costs. But this..." I rub at my forehead, even though there's no headache. "I can help her. I have resources she doesn't. I'm going to make her see reason."

"Do you think you can? I can only tell you this." Luke pulls out of the garage, and we begin the drive. "When I was messed up, I didn't understand what love was. But once I got off the booze, and once I fell in love with Katelyn, I didn't want her anywhere near me. I left her. I left her in Manhattan and came to LA so I could take care of my past. I had to do it to be worthy of her. The last thing I wanted was for her to get involved. This was on me, and I couldn't risk her being harmed."

He knows. Luke fucking knows.

He left Katelyn.

He loved her, yet he left her.

"Turns out she got involved anyway," I say.

"She did, but not because it was anything *I* wanted."

"There's a difference between you and Aspen, though," I say. "You went back to take care of a situation that was your own doing. Aspen is innocent. She hasn't done anything wrong."

"No, she hasn't. And you're right. The situations *are* different. But the emotions aren't. She knows she may find trouble, and she wants you far away from that."

Fuck it all. "What's the answer then?"

"The answer is we go get her. Because she's just one woman. Granted, she's a *strong* woman, but what else does she have working for her? Not your contacts and not mine."

I resist the urge to grab at my hair and pull it. "Why? Why would she try to do this on her own? She's not thinking clearly."

"No, she's not. She's thinking through the red eyes of vengeance and rage. Believe me. I've been there. I know."

"You think I *haven't* been there? Talk to me when you've been starved and tortured and beaten."

That's as far as I'll go. I won't give Luke the grisly details.

"She's been through much of the same," Luke says.

"You think I don't know that? I want to save her from ever having to go through any of that shit again. That's I why wanted to leave all of this in the past. It's not worth dredging it all up."

"It is to her."

His words crush me like a fucking anvil.

All I want is what's best for Aspen. I want her safe. I want her to have a good life. A life that's so wonderful it makes up for those five years she lost.

But is that my decision to make?

I have a vested interest. I love her. I want to build a life with her. Have children with her someday.

It is to her.

Then it is to me as well.

"I see you understand," Luke says.

"I haven't said a damned word."

"It was a look on your face. You went from rigid to only slightly tense."

"You saw that in my face?"

"During my years underground, I learned to read people. That's part of why I was so successful."

"Yeah? We learn to read people in the Navy too."

"This isn't a contest, Buck. For God's sake. You're making everything about you and me. About our past. About Emily. This isn't about any of that."

God, could I hate this guy more? Except that I'm starting to like him, and I fucking hate that. I also fucking hate that's he's making sense.

"We don't have to be friends," Luke continues. "It's probably impossible. But we do have to work together. This is as important to me as it is to you. Because it's important to Katelyn and Aspen."

"You'll never understand."

"That's where you're wrong. I *do* understand. If I were in your shoes, I'd hate me too. I have a sister you know."

"You do?"

"Yeah, her name is Alexandra. We call her Sandy. I have a brother too. Both younger than I am. I love them the way you love Emily."

"Yeah? And what would you do if someone did to your sister what you did to Emily?"

"I'd want to fucking kill him."

"Don't tempt me."

"I would never like him. And no, I wouldn't kill him. That would be murder, and I don't want to spend the rest of my life behind bars. But I would never trust him. I would never accept him. It would be damned hard to accept his help when I needed it."

"So you get it."

"I do. But I would *take* the help. I would take that help for the woman I love. That's what you're going to do as well."

"We've been through this. I already said I'd work with you. I'd accept your help."

"Then stop fighting it. I know it's hard. Really, I do. But we've got to work together. You've got to stop fighting me on every fucking thing."

He's right. This isn't about him or about me. Or about Emily or about our past.

It's about Aspen, pure and simple. About what's best for Aspen. And that is Luke and me working together.

"I'll try."

"You've got to do better than try, man. This is your woman we're talking about. I can't change my past. I would if I could, but I can't. All I can do is be the best man I know how to be *now*, in the present. To do the best I can for you and for Aspen."

"Fine." I purse my lips.

Luke pulls into the rental car place.

My body tingles.

Aspen is here.

I open the passenger door and am out of the car before he even stops. I race into the rental car place. "I'm looking for Aspen Davis."

The clerk gestures to someone who must be the boss.

He comes toward me. "Are you Mr. Ashton?"

"No. That's him." I point to Luke as he enters. "I'm Buck Moreno."

"I'm Luke Ashton."

"Mr. Ashton. Ms. Davis is in the back room."

"How did you keep her there?" I ask.

"We just said there was some extended paperwork because she had an out-of-town driver's license."

"And she bought that?"

"She didn't have a choice. She wasn't going to get a rental car."

Ants scamper through my body. I need to see Aspen, and I need to see her now. "Just take us to her. Please."

"Right away."

Luke and I walk around the back of the counter and follow the manager to a back room. Aspen is sitting, her back to us, facing a desk.

Without turning around, she says, "Finally. Can we get on with this please?"

"Aspen," I say, my voice a growl.

She looks over her shoulder, rises, her eyes wide. "Buck! What are you doing here?" Then she turns to the manager. "What the hell have you done?"

"Aspen, what are you doing?" I ask. "I don't understand."

Luke glances at the manager. "Could we give them some privacy, please?"

"Sure, Mr. Ashton." The manager leaves.

Luke follows him, closing the door behind him.

"I just..." Aspen shakes her head, her voice shaking. "Please, Buck. Just let me do what I have to do."

"No. Did you really think you could get away with this?

You do know that Luke has top-notch security. His camera saw you go."

Aspen closes her eyes and sighs. "I thought I found them all last night. And I tried to be so quiet."

"You could've been quiet as a mouse, baby, and Luke's security would've seen you go."

"How did you know I was here?"

"One of the guards followed you."

She huffs. "That's a total invasion of my privacy."

"Yeah," Buck says, "and I don't give a rat's ass. I'm glad Luke has such good security. I'm glad we followed you. Because who knows what kind of trouble you would've gotten into otherwise?"

Aspen narrows her eyes. "Don't treat me like I'm some kind of fool."

"You're not a fool, baby. No one thinks you are. But we all love you, and we want to protect you. Let us help you."

She sighs. "I was never going to get away with this, was I?"

Buck shakes his head. "No. Not on my watch."

I grab Aspen and pull her to me. She melts into my arms and lets out a choking sob.

"I'm sorry," she says.

"I really ought to shake some sense into you."

Any anger I felt is overshadowed by pure relief. I'm so happy she's safe. So glad we got to her in time.

"I'd tell you I'm sorry," Aspen says, "but I'm not, Buck. I love you too much to drag you into this."

"I'm already in it, baby. And right now I'm so fucking relieved that you're okay. But part of me is angry and hurt. Why don't you trust me?"

"Are you kidding? I trust you more than I trust anyone. I trust you with my life, Buck."

“Then why did you run?”

“I told you. Because I love you. I can’t have your safety put in jeopardy because of me. Look at what’s happened to you already. You were knocked unconscious and left to bleed out and die. Two people are dead. Gloria and her husband. Dead people are following me around, Buck. I desperately don’t want you to be one of them.”

14

ASPEN

What else can I say?

It's the whole truth. It's why I don't want my father involved in this. Why I don't want Katelyn and Luke involved in this.

And mostly why I don't want Buck involved in this.

He doesn't say anything.

But he's angry and hurt. It's pouring off him in waves.

He thinks I don't trust him when the opposite is true.

It's the others I don't trust. I trust *him* with my life. I trust him to stand in front of a bullet for me.

And that's exactly why I don't want him caught up in this.

"Let's go," he says.

"Buck..."

"No arguments. Not a fucking one." He grips my shoulders. "I'm serious. This is over. We're in this together, Aspen. Nothing you can say or do will change that."

I sigh. There's nothing more I can say, so I leave with Buck. We meet Luke in the parking lot and head home in his Tesla.

Back at the beach house, Edgar greets me. I pick him up and kiss his soft head. I missed this little fellow, and I wasn't even gone that long. Jed is happy to see me too, and I give him loves and snuggles as well.

But it's Katelyn... Katelyn comes to me, and she's not happy. She's not smiling. "How could you do this? How could you worry us like this?"

Apparently there was no reason for her to be worried. Luke knew where I was the whole time.

But I understand. I understand that she's angry. She's feeling much the same way Buck is feeling.

She thinks I don't trust her.

When the opposite is true.

I could argue with her. I could tell her my reasoning on everything, and I open my mouth to do so—

But all that comes out is, "I'm sorry."

She launches herself at me and gives me a bear hug. "Don't ever do this again. Haven't we spent enough of our lives worrying about each other?"

Is she talking about the island?

Did she truly worry about others on the island?

The island was a funny place. We didn't make friends. We couldn't. Because in the back of our minds we always hoped one of the others got chosen instead of us on any given night.

Hoping for the pain-and-suffering of a friend... Yeah, doesn't really work that way.

So we weren't friends.

We didn't discuss what happened to us when we went out on the hunt.

Perhaps Katelyn considered that we were friends because we were two of the three who sometimes sat in the common room and watched the old sitcoms on the TV.

But we didn't talk.

We only started talking at the retreat center and then in Manhattan. And even then, we didn't truly talk until we went out for coffee that one time.

Still, I look at her now, and she *is* my best friend. I've never had a friend who cares quite as much as Katelyn.

"I won't," I promise.

This time I mean it.

I won't go off on my own again.

If it hurts these people I care about that much, then I'm not accomplishing what I set out to do—which was keep them out of danger, but also out of pain.

"I need to tell you all something, though," I continue.

"What is it?" Katelyn asks.

"I'm not backing down."

Buck opens his mouth to speak, but I hold up a hand.

"I know your feelings on the matter, Buck, and I respect them. I respect all of you so much. Which is why I didn't want to lead you into any danger. I love you all. But this is something I have to do. In the marrow of my bones I know it. I have to see justice served."

"Baby..."

"No, Buck. I know how you feel. I know you think it's better for me to just get over it."

"Aspen," Buck says, "I know it's not that simple. You don't just *get over* things. Post-traumatic stress disorder is a real thing. I of all people should know that."

"You can't bring the people who harmed you to justice," I tell him. "They're in another country. And for all we know they could be dead by now anyway. But the people who harmed me? They're here. And they're alive. They've killed two people, and they tried to kill you too. We have to bring them down, Buck. We can't let them be outside walking the streets. Who knows who else they will harm?"

Buck lets out a sigh.

A really big sigh.

A huge part of him understands. He always has.

"Maybe I don't get a vote here—" Luke begins.

"That's right. You don't." From Buck.

"But," Luke continues, "I agree with Aspen. These people need to be brought down. And you agree with me too, Moreno."

Buck says nothing.

"Yeah. That's proof that you agree." A smile of satisfaction slides over Luke's face.

"Fine," Buck says. "I agree. We need to find these motherfuckers. But why don't you and I do it? Let's leave the ladies out of it."

"No way." I move between Buck and Luke. "I'm the one who was wronged all these years. I will not be treated like a little woman here. I'm as tough as any of you people."

What a crock. I'm six feet tall, an athlete, and full of muscle. But I'm not as tough as a Navy SEAL or a former underground drug lord.

I know it, and everyone else here knows it. They're nice enough not to contradict me though.

Toughness aside, I do know how to protect myself.

My father taught me long ago.

"I'm going to need a gun," I say.

Both Buck's and Luke's eyes nearly pop out of their sockets.

"I can shoot a gun. You know who my father is, Buck.

You've seen the gun collection in our basement. Do you really think he never taught me how to handle a piece?"

"I can get you set up," Luke says.

"What do you have available?" Buck asks.

"A few Glocks, a few Smith & Wesson's. I'm thinking a nine-millimeter for her."

"I'm standing right here," I say. "And yes, a nine-millimeter would be perfect."

"Okay," Buck says. "Show us what you've got."

An hour later, I'm armed with a Smith & Wesson CSX. It feels good in my hands and strapped to my shoulder with the holster Luke fitted on me.

"We should go to the shooting range," Buck says.

"We can if you want," I tell him, "but I'm a great shot."

"I'm sure you are, but when is the last time you actually held a gun in your hand?"

I bite my lip. He makes a good point. So many times I wished for a damned gun when I was on the island.

It's been five years or more.

"Point taken." I turn to Luke. "Where can we practice shooting around here?"

"I know of a few shooting ranges in the area," Luke says. "That's not what I would recommend, though."

Buck clears his throat. "What do you recommend then?"

"I'll take you to my father's mansion. He has a shooting range in the basement."

"What?" Buck says.

"My grandfather was a bit of a nutcase. He built an entire underground bunker. In fact, that's where I stayed when I came back to LA because there was a high price on my head."

"You have an underground bunker," Buck says, his tone noncommittal.

"Yeah. I'm pretty sure that's what I just said."

Buck shoves his hands in the pockets of his jeans. "Okay. What the fuck? Let's go shoot some guns."

15

BUCK

Damn it all to hell.

Lucifer Ashton Junior has a fucking shooting range in his basement, complete with a control booth, target retrieval carriers, and four shooting booths. The walls are concrete blocks and the ceiling concrete and steel.

One of the nicest ranges I've ever seen, at that.

"How's the ventilation down here?" I ask Luke.

"State of the art," he says. "My father never does anything half-assed. Except when it comes to parenting, but that's another story."

Yeah. One I don't want to hear at the moment, and one I'm pretty sure he doesn't want to tell. "Good. I'm not feeling the need to inhale any combustion byproducts today."

"You won't," he says.

Katelyn is with us, at Luke's request. She's never shot a gun before, and her nerves are a complete mess.

But she's Luke's problem.

Aspen is mine.

She turns out to not be a problem at all. The woman is a crack shot.

Of course she was trained by the best—her SEAL father.

"You're amazing," I tell her.

"I was always pretty good. I'm surprising myself, though, since it's been so long."

"Some things are like riding a bike," I say. "Apparently shooting is one of them."

"Then why did you insist we practice?"

"Because I have your best interests at heart, Aspen. You haven't had a gun in your hands for nearly six years. I wanted to make sure you could still handle it."

"Well, I proved that I can."

"Yes, you have. Physically, you are as adept as anyone I've seen with a gun."

"Physically?" She raises an eyebrow.

I don't want to get into this with her, but do I have a choice? My job is to take care of her, and making sure she's okay is part of that. "I'm a little worried about your emotional state. You're so set on vengeance. And with a gun in your hand..."

"For God's sake, Buck. Give me a little credit. I'm not a moron."

"Did I say that?"

"You just accused me of being emotionally unstable."

"No I didn't, but tell me something," I say. "If you knew for sure who set you up, and if that person came within shooting distance of you right at this moment, are you telling me you could hold yourself back?"

She doesn't reply.

Good. I've struck a nerve.

I love this woman, but I know how it feels to take another

human life. It doesn't matter if that human was a piece of shit and the whole world is better off with him in hell where he belongs.

It's still taking a life, and to a person with a good heart, like Aspen? Well, the effects will be long lasting. I should know.

"I'm good," she says. "I could go for the leg. The shoulder. I know how to stop a person without ending his life."

"You're that good? Could you hit a moving target?"

No response again.

"Look. You *are* good. You hit your bull's-eye every time. Your hand is as steady as any surgeon's. You're almost as good as I am, baby, and that's a pretty damned big compliment coming from me. But even I don't labor under the delusion that I can hit a moving target right where I want to."

"You were a sniper."

"I was. And I never missed. But I was very careful not to take the shot until the target was standing still."

She sighs. "You've made your point."

"Good. This firearm is for your protection. Not for you to take revenge on who wronged you."

"I get it."

"Good. It's okay to feel like you want to kill them. You're human. Believe me. I understand. But to do so won't make your life better, Aspen. It will make it worse. The best thing we can do is catch these people and make sure they're put away for a long time."

"You're right."

Does she believe me? I think she does, rationally.

But she's still so bent on vengeance.

And God…I've been there.

"Promise me," I say.

"I will. I'll promise you whatever you need. Because that's how much I love you, Buck, and that's how much I know, in my heart, that you're looking out for me."

I cup her cheek then, run my thumb over her luscious lower lip. "Promise me you'll keep your head. You won't let your emotions run wild. That you'll only use this gun to protect your life or the life of someone else."

"I promise." Her voice is strong, her countenance rigid.

She means it.

I just hope, if push comes to shove, she'll remember.

"I want to see how Katelyn is doing," she says.

Katelyn and Luke left the shooting range a while ago. We find Katelyn sitting, her head in her hands, Luke with his arm around her.

"What's wrong?" Aspen asks.

Katelyn raises her head. Tears stain her cheeks. "I'm okay. It was just a lot to process, after everything. Holding a gun. Shooting a gun."

"The first time is pretty daunting," Aspen agrees.

"It's more than daunting."

"I suppose. I was only ten the first time I shot a gun, and yes, it was daunting, but it was also really cool. I got to be like my dad, who was the coolest person in the world to me at that point."

"I guess I just never thought of myself as someone who would ever have to use a gun," Katelyn says. "Even now, which makes no sense at all, considering what I've been through."

"It's for your own safety, sweetheart," Luke says.

"I know. And I'll get better."

"Of course you will," Luke says. "This was just your first

time. But this is important. I want you to be able to defend yourself."

"Believe me, I want that too," Katelyn replies. "I don't ever want to get taken again."

"You won't be, if I have anything to say about it." Luke shakes his head. "We have great security at home. But just on the off chance..."

Katelyn nods.

"It's actually a pretty funny thing, Katelyn," I tell her. "Once you get used to it, and once you realize you have control over the firearm—that it's not some weapon that will just go off without you knowing it—it's very empowering."

"Maybe *you* should teach me, Aspen."

"Actually, that's a really good idea," Luke says. "She was a little freaked out with me."

"I'll be happy to," Aspen says, "once we've resolved everything else."

"That's fine." Luke nods. "Katelyn's going to be kept out of harm's way while the three of us find these people."

"But I want to help," Katelyn says.

"You will. But you're not going to be on the frontlines," Luke says. "Not until you're comfortable with the firearm."

Katelyn relents then. "Okay."

AFTER LUNCH, I finally get a shower. Then Luke, Aspen, and I meet in his office for a strategy session.

"I feel bad for Katelyn," Aspen says.

"She's okay," Luke says. "She wants to help, but until she's better at protecting herself—"

"She did a pretty good job of protecting herself when you were in trouble," I say.

"She did, but she confided in me later that in order to do that, she had to become Moonstone again."

Aspen bites her lip. "It's hard for me to imagine the way Katelyn dealt with things on the island. She told me about it once. One time she was punished, and she was..." Aspen shakes her head. "I don't know the specifics. I don't *want* to know the specifics. But the punishment was so harsh that she had to push Katelyn aside and become Moonstone. She made herself over, became something that could survive in that place. She nearly didn't even remember her own name when we were rescued."

"But you remembered." I say.

"We dealt with things differently. Aspen and Garnet were pretty much the same person. Once I got rescued, I repressed a lot of the memories. Hell, I didn't even recognize the SEAL Trident on your arm and back, Buck. And that was a memory from before my time on the island."

"The human mind is a strange thing," Luke says.

"It is," I agree.

Which is one of the main reasons I'm so worried about Aspen. I don't want her to go off halfcocked and do something she may regret.

"Have you checked in with the Wolfes lately?" Luke asks me.

Crap. "No, I haven't. Getting hit on the head and spending time in the hospital kind of got in the way of that."

"You should check in with them, Buck," Aspen says. "They'll want to know that we're okay."

"I will. Right now."

I send Reid a quick text to let him know where we are and what we're about to do.

Anything you need, he texts back.

Good.

It's nice to have the financial backing.

"All right," Luke says, "I've got good news and bad news."

"Give us the good news first," I say.

"I found Taylor Wallace."

"Okay. That's good," Aspen says. "We can talk to her."

"The bad news is she refuses to talk to us."

"Which means she must have something to hide," I say.

"That would be my guess. I'm thinking we go see her anyway."

"Is she here in town?"

"She actually lives in Reseda."

"Reseda? Isn't she an heiress?"

"Apparently not anymore. Daddy cut her off."

"Why would he do that?" Aspen asks.

"That," Luke says, "is what we need to find out."

16

ASPEN

I'm armed.

I'm constantly aware of the pistol strapped to my side, under my T-shirt.

I'm actually wearing one of Buck's T-shirts to hide the holster. All of mine are too tight.

Buck uses an ankle holster for his piece.

I can't do that. Not in LA, when I'm wearing shorts. I don't know how Buck exists wearing jeans all the time. I'm pretty sure we're both breaking the California concealed carry laws, but I don't give a shit.

Buck and I are on our way to see Taylor Wallace.

It's Friday. I actually had to check my phone to see what day it was. Crazy stuff.

Taylor Wallace, heiress to Wallace Leathers.

What does she have to do with this? Something, clearly, or she wouldn't refuse to speak to us. Taylor was sitting in the aisle seat across from me on the flight to Manhattan. If someone slipped something into my drink, she's definitely a suspect.

Will she even be home? If her father truly did cut her off, she's probably working.

She's married, and her wife's name is Margo Caprice. Maybe one of them will be home.

More likely not.

We drive up to the condominium complex. Taylor lives in a corner unit, and we park outside the front of it.

"What if she's not home?" I ask.

"I brought supplies."

I look in the back of the rental car. Sure enough, there's Buck's little black bag. Inside are his lockpicking tools and the blue nitrile gloves that we used at Gloria's place.

God...

I really don't want to walk in and find more dead people.

Or another dog to take care of.

I raise my hand and knock on the door. Then I stand out of the way, so if someone looks out for people, they see Buck, not me.

Nothing.

I knock again, and this time, the door cracks open.

"Yes?"

The voice.

Is it Taylor Wallace? I have no idea. I knew her so long ago, and we weren't close.

"Hi," Buck says. "I'm Buck Moreno. I'd like to talk to you about Aspen Davis."

"I have nothing to say to you."

The woman closes the door, but quick as a flash, Buck's Army boot slides between the door and the frame, blocking her from shutting it.

"We need to talk to you. It's important."

I come into view then. "Hello, Taylor."

I say her name before I actually recognize her, but yes, it is her. Taylor Wallace. Her hair is dark now with blue tips where it used to be blond, and it's shoulder length instead of long and tied back. But her light brown eyes penetrate me. Those eyes that I recognize. This is Taylor.

She raises her eyebrows. "Thank God you're all right. We thought you were dead!"

I totally don't buy the look of mock surprise on her face. "Yeah. Rumors of my death were premature."

She's definitely hiding something. Those years on the island did a lot for my intuition, and it's not failing me now. Gloria swore Taylor wasn't involved—that Taylor's wasn't one of the voices she heard in the locker room—but Gloria ended up dead.

"This is where you invite us in," I say.

"I don't have anything to say to either of you."

"Your long-lost teammate shows up, someone who you thought was dead, and you have *nothing* to say? You just thanked God that I'm okay."

"It's not that. It's my...my wife."

"Is she home?"

"Well...no."

"What? She doesn't like you to have visitors?" This from Buck.

"Nothing like that."

"Then let us in," I say. "You have information that we need."

"I don't have any information you could possibly need."

"Then why are you refusing to talk to us?"

"Because... It just brings back so many...bad memories."

"What kind of bad memories?"

"You know... Gloria..."

"Gloria's dead," Buck says.

Taylor's hand goes to her mouth, and as she backs away from the door, Buck takes advantage of her movement and lets us both in.

As much as I thought Taylor was feigning before, this surprise seems real.

I ease her toward the couch in the living room and push her gently into a sitting position. I sit down next to her.

"You didn't know."

She shakes her head.

"Whatever happened between you and Gloria, Taylor?"

"It wasn't pretty," Taylor says. "After Gloria got your position on the team, she changed."

"What do you mean?"

"She got kind of full of herself. She decided she was too good for me."

"What? That's ridiculous. That's not Gloria at all."

Taylor shrugs. "Maybe I knew her better than you. We were in a relationship after all."

I shake my head. "Gloria told me you broke up because you didn't have much in common.

"I guess we didn't. She's bisexual, you know."

I nod. "Yeah, I know."

"At that point, she decided it was better PR for her to be with a man than a woman. So we broke up."

"And that upset you."

"Well, of course it did. I was in love with her."

"She didn't mention that you were upset by the breakup," I say.

"It doesn't really matter what she told you," Taylor says. "*I'm* telling you the truth."

"And how convenient that she isn't here to discredit you."

"Look, my volleyball days are way behind me. They ended in heartache. I lost Gloria, and I lost my inheritance."

"How does volleyball have anything to do with your inheritance?" I ask.

"It's a long story."

"Lucky for you," Buck says, "we're free, and we love a good long story."

She sighs. "I really can't talk to you about this."

"We can subpoena you," Buck says.

"Don't you have to file a lawsuit for that?"

"The lawsuits are already filed," Buck says. "By the Wolfe family on behalf of the young women. Aspen being one of them."

This is news to me.

But then I realize what Buck's doing. He's lying to Taylor. No one has filed any kind of lawsuit. I mean seriously, why would the Wolfes file the suits? We'd have to file them with the Wolfes backing us.

But maybe Taylor will buy it.

"Fine. Then subpoena me."

"Will do," Buck rises. "Come on, Aspen. We'll be back with the subpoena in a few hours."

Oh no. We're not going anywhere. She'll fly.

Buck must know this.

He does.

He goes to the door and secures the deadbolt.

"What are you doing?" Taylor asks.

"Change of plans. We're going to get the information we want *now*. You'll get your subpoena later. But we're here now, and we need to know what you know."

Taylor sighs. "All right. Fine. Sit back down."

We do.

Taylor rises. "I'll get us some coffee."

"That would be nice." I say.

She walks out of the living room.

"Follow her," Buck says.

"Why?"

"Trust me."

I rise and follow her, and lo and behold—

Taylor is about to walk through a sliding glass door that leads to her backyard.

I grab her arm. "Going somewhere?"

She shakes herself free. "You can't imprison me in my own home."

"I think we just did."

"That's a crime, you know."

"Are you going to call a cop?"

"You can't—"

"Look, I've got nothing against you, assuming you had nothing to do with what happened to me. But if you did? You're going to pay one way or the other. The only way I'll go even slightly easy on you is if you tell me everything you know right now."

"It wasn't my idea," Taylor says.

"What wasn't your idea?"

"Any of it."

"So you knew? You knew what they did to me?"

"No! Of course not. You really think I would do anything like that?"

"I don't know what the fuck to think right now, Taylor. You won't talk to me, and the few things you are saying are full of contradictions. So that leads me to believe that you orchestrated at least part of it."

"No. Nothing like that."

"You're going to come back to the living room now, and you're going to tell us everything."

"You have to protect me, then."

"I'll decide whether to protect you after you tell me what you know."

"No, you *have* to. Gloria's dead. You told me yourself."

"What makes you think that has anything to do with me?"

"How can it not? All of a sudden you come here asking for information. And now Gloria's dead."

She's right, of course. Gloria is dead because of me. But Gloria obviously knew something she didn't tell me. Why else would she be dead?

And Taylor... Maybe I do have a duty to protect her. But not until I find out what she knows.

17

BUCK

Aspen and Taylor return to the living room.

"Was I right, or was I right?" I ask.

"You were right," Aspen says. "Sit down, Taylor."

"So you tried to make a break for it," I say to Taylor.

"Can you blame me?"

"Not in the slightest. But I'm sure Aspen filled you in on what we need."

"I need your protection first."

"Fine. Done."

Aspen looks at me, raises her eyebrows slightly. I nod back at her. Very slightly.

What the hell? We probably should've offered Gloria protection. But at the time, we weren't sure whether she was a friend or an enemy.

I think she was probably a bit of both.

Probably the same as this woman sitting on the couch now.

She's nervous and fidgety. A nice-looking woman, not

quite as tall as Aspen, with dark hair highlighted in blue and light brown eyes. Her hair is short, although not as short as Aspen's. She's still clearly athletic, as she's wearing yoga pants and a sports bra.

"Where's your wife today?" I ask.

"She's at work. Why?"

"I don't really want anyone barging in on us right now."

"She gets home around six. She's a software engineer."

"What do you do?"

"I'm an assistant coach for a local volleyball team. We practice in the evenings."

"Good. Then you're free for now."

Taylor nods. "That's why I'm home."

"All right. We will guarantee your protection. I have the backing of the Wolfe family in Manhattan, and they have offered Aspen and me everything we need to find out the truth behind her abduction."

"All right."

Interesting. No look of surprise on Taylor's face when I use the word *abduction*.

That's a big tell.

"Where do you want me to start?" she asks.

"At the beginning," I say.

"Like I said, it's a long story. It starts before Aspen even joined the team."

"So was Gloria in my position before I joined?"

"They had all but promised it to her," Taylor says. "But then they found you."

"Okay."

"Gloria was just as good as you," Taylor says. "You got the position because of your size."

"I don't think that was ever a secret," Aspen says.

"No, it wasn't."

"Gloria and I were pretty much equal as far as skill goes," Aspen says. "I always knew that, and so did she."

"So then you can understand why she was upset. The position was all but hers, but because you were a few inches taller, you got it."

"It may interest you to know that I have no control over my genetics," Aspen says.

"We all get that. Nobody had anything against you as a person. Especially not Gloria. She loved everyone, or she tried to. It ate her up inside, how you made her feel."

"What?" Aspen's jaw drops.

"According to Aspen," I say, "Gloria never had a bad word to say about anyone. She prayed for everyone."

"That's exactly how she was," Taylor says. "But she felt a lot of resentment toward you, Aspen. And she hated herself for it. It tore her up."

"I never saw any of that. We were thrown together all the time for practice. For hotel stays."

"She never *let* you see it. She never let most people see it. But she and I were in a relationship. So I *did* see it."

"Did she talk to you about it?" I ask.

"Not at first. I had to drag it out of her."

"And how did it come out?" Aspen asks.

"It was about a week before we went to that Manhattan game. When they announced that you and she would be rooming together yet again. She asked the manager to change the assignments. She wanted to room with me, or really with anyone besides you. But they wouldn't change it. So Gloria... She just... She wasn't herself, and I asked her what was wrong. And finally she just blurted it out."

"Blurted *what* out exactly?" I ask.

"How she hated the fact that she was constantly reminded of how she was second-best. And now she had to room with you again."

"Wait, wait, wait. This was only like the second or third time we had a room together."

"Because it was only the second or third time since you had taken her position on the team."

"I had just joined the team. I had just graduated from college."

"Yeah, that's what I mean. You took the position that she was supposed to get."

"You keep saying I took something from her. I didn't. I *earned* that position. I tried out. I jumped through all the hoops just like she did."

"And you got the position because you're a few inches taller than she is."

"Did I not just say I know that? That I admit we were equal in every way *except* that? We could both jump, but I could jump higher because I'm taller. And did I also not just say that I have no control over my height? My height brought something to the table that Gloria didn't have. Is that *my* fault?" Aspen clenches her fists and her cheeks redden.

"Baby..."

I don't want to upset Aspen, but she's getting emotional. And that needs to stop. Especially with a gun strapped to her shoulder.

She seems to understand. She closes her mouth.

I clear my throat. "Taylor, this is important. Once you found out how Gloria truly felt about Aspen, what happened then?"

"She cried. She bawled her eyes out over the fact that she tried so hard to be a good person, but she had these feelings of utter resentment toward another human being. And it wasn't that she didn't like you, Aspen. She did. She loved you, even. It wasn't that. It's that she hated herself for the feelings she was having."

Aspen chews on her bottom lip. Good. This is bothering her, but she's controlled. She's not simply full of rage.

"So you were the only one who knew how she truly felt?" I say.

"At first, yes."

I raise my eyebrows. "At first?"

She nods. "Yeah. I guess that's where I come in."

Aspen stops chewing on her lip, and her eyes take on a different look. She narrows them, and her features tighten.

I spoke too soon.

There's the anger.

"Exactly what are you saying?" Aspen asks.

"I may have let it slip how Gloria really felt."

"To whom?" Aspen says, gritting her teeth.

"You have to understand. Everyone loved Gloria because Gloria loved everyone."

"I know that," I say. "Aspen described her as the Miss Congeniality of the team."

"You did?" Taylor looks at Aspen.

"Yeah, I did. I loved Gloria too. Everyone did. She never had a bad word to say about anyone, and she always looked on the bright side."

"That's how she made it look, anyway," Taylor says.

I clear my throat again. "Go on, please."

"I was talking to another person on the team."

"Search your memory bank," Aspen says without emotion.

"She was a setter."

"Nancy Mosely?"

Taylor fidgets with her hands. "Right, that's it. Nancy Mosely."

"Nancy was a nice person."

"She and I were talking, and it just kind of came out about how Gloria really felt."

"You're not going to tell me Nancy was behind this."

"No." Taylor shakes her head. "Someone overheard us talking."

"Who?"

"I don't know. All I know is that we heard them leave the locker room when we were done talking."

"So it didn't occur to you to check and see if anyone was in there who could overhear you?"

"It wasn't like that. It's not like we were having some kind of secret talk. We were just chatting, and it came out. You remember Nancy. She was a nice person. She talked to everyone."

"Tell me about Nancy," I say.

"Are you talking to me?" Aspen asks.

"I'm talking to whichever one of you who can tell me a little bit more about Nancy Mosely."

Aspen wrinkles her forehead. "She was nice. She was a setter. But she was also a good middle blocker, and she loved playing that position. But she wasn't as good at it as Gloria and I were."

"So that means you, she, and Gloria would practice together sometimes," I say.

"Yeah. We did."

"All right. So she was familiar with both of you."

"Right. She would've been."

"Do either of you have any idea where she is now?"

"Buck, I don't have any idea where any of them are now. As you know."

"Right. Do you know where to find her, Taylor?"

Taylor looks down at her lap. "No. I have no idea where to find her."

That's a lie.

I clear my throat again. "Wrong. You *do* know how to find her."

Taylor looks up at me then, her eyes wide. "No. I just said I didn't."

"And you also looked at your lap when you said it. It's a classic tell."

Shit. I'm so angry and anxious to find out who is behind all this for Aspen's sake, that I just made a major blunder.

I shouldn't have mentioned the classic tell. Now she'll force herself not to do it.

"My guess is," I go on, "that you just pretended not to remember Nancy's name."

"You're wrong," Taylor gasps. "I would never—"

"Save it." From Aspen. "Do you have any idea what I went through? After they took me? Look at my legs, Taylor. I notice you haven't looked at me directly since we got here. Look at the scars on my legs."

Taylor closes her eyes.

"Open your fucking eyes," I tell her, "and look at what you helped make happen."

18

ASPEN

She can't.

Taylor seems to be physically unable to gaze at my legs. I've half a mind to strip in front of her so she can see the whip marks on my back, my missing nipple.

But there are enough scars on my legs for now. Especially... God, I can't go there.

For a moment, Buck rises, and for another moment, I think he's going to physically force Taylor to look at me.

But he doesn't touch her.

Buck is a good man. He knows when to back off.

This is my territory. I will *make* her look.

I rise and stand in front of her, so she has to actually close her eyes to avoid looking at my thighs.

My thighs, which have whip marks, stab wounds. But my thighs are nothing compared to my calf.

Taylor gasps out a sob.

"Save your tears," I say. "God knows I had to save mine."

"I'm so sorry," Taylor says. "None of us ever meant to—"

"Stop right there," Buck says. "We don't really give a rat's ass what you meant or didn't mean to have happen. You clearly know what's going on, and that's what we need to know."

"Nancy..." I say. "It's all starting to make sense. If Gloria got my position, Nancy would be her backup. It would cement her place on the team in the position she desired."

Taylor sniffles. "I suppose so, but you really think Nancy could've done any of this?"

"Really?" I say. "You're going to go back there? Just tell us what the fuck happened, Taylor."

"You don't understand," she says. "I lost everything because of this. My father disinherited me. I lost everything."

"Save your fucking whining. You didn't lose what *I* lost."

This time I do it. I remove my T-shirt. Throw it on the couch. Then I pull Taylor into a stand. Force her to look at me.

Her gaze zeroes in on the pistol strapped to my shoulder.

I don't mention the gun, and neither does she. I simply turn, show myself at every angle.

"Do you see the scars? They whipped me. So badly sometimes that I got infected, and I nearly died."

I turn around, unclasp my bra, and let it fall from my shoulders. From one shoulder actually. The holster holds the other side in place. But it's enough to show her what they did to me.

"But that wasn't the worst part. Take a look at my breasts, Taylor. Take a long, close look."

She bursts into tears. "I'm so sorry, Aspen."

"For God's sake, don't be sorry. Just *help* me. Help me bring these people to justice."

She falls back on the couch. Buck helps me reposition the bra and clasp it, and then I pull his T-shirt over my head.

Taylor sobs.

I look toward Buck. He shrugs. Right. He doesn't know how to handle a sobbing woman.

Unless she's me. He does well with me. But I don't think I want him taking Taylor up to her bathroom and running her a lavender bath.

No, I need to take the lead here.

I need to deal with a sobbing Taylor Wallace—who was disinherited by her millionaire father and who clearly had something to do with my abduction.

I let her sob. I let her sob for five minutes and then ten.

But now it's time to stop.

I grip her shoulders and force her to turn toward me on the couch. "Snap out of it, now. You had your time to weep. If I can get through this without breaking down, so can you."

She chokes back one last sob and nods. "You're right. Of course, you're right."

"Start talking now," Buck says. "We've been more than patient."

"All right. But you need to know that the reason I tried to leave the back way isn't because I know anything more."

"Why was it then?"

"I need to protect someone."

"All right," Buck says. "You've got my attention. I understand what that feels like. Who do you need to protect?"

"I need to start at the beginning," Taylor says.

Meanwhile Buck is fiddling with his phone. He must be researching something or talking to Reid Wolfe. It's my job now to keep Taylor occupied while he finds out whatever he's trying to find out.

"Go on then," I say to Taylor.

"I really loved Gloria," she says.

"What does that have to do with anything?"

"It means... I was in love with her. I thought she was the one. I know we were young back then, but she was so good. Such a good person."

"That's what I always thought."

"Like I said, we broke up soon after you disappeared. She gave me the PR excuse, and she also said that she had to concentrate on the team now that she was the middle blocker. She didn't have time for a relationship."

For God's sake. I've heard Taylor's tale of breakup woe. But at least she's talking. "Maybe she was telling the truth," I say.

"Maybe. I don't know."

"Did she have any other relationships while she was still on the team?"

"Not with team members." Taylor cocks her head. "Come to think of it, not with anyone else, that I know of."

"Then she was probably telling you the truth," I say. "She wanted to give her all to the team. The PR thing probably stung you a little. I get that."

"All I knew was that the person who I thought was the love of my life basically left me for a job."

"Then she wasn't the love of your life."

"Of course she wasn't. But that's how I felt at the time."

"I can understand that."

At that time I thought Brandon was the love of my life. Turns out I was very wrong.

"All right. So you and Gloria broke up, and then what happened?"

"There were others," she says. "Others who had more to do with this than I did. Gloria for one."

"Not buying. Gloria's not here to defend herself, and we all remember what kind of person she was."

Taylor clears her throat. "Others. On the team."

"Laura and Celeste by any chance?"

Taylor raises her eyebrows and then nods. "Right. Laura and Celeste."

"Nice try. I'm not buying. They were a couple of bad seeds, but they weren't involved in this."

"But they—"

"Taylor," I say, "get to the fucking point. You're obviously not above selling out someone else, so get to it."

"Well—"

We all jerk as the front door opens.

A woman walks in, Taylor's wife, presumably, except—

I drop my jaw.

"Nancy Mosely?"

19

BUCK

Now we're getting somewhere.

Margo Caprice...or Nancy Mosely... Whoever the fuck she is, she's also a tall and athletic type, but still not as tall as Aspen. She's dressed in a pantsuit, and her dirty blond hair is pulled back into a professional looking bun. She's not as attractive as Taylor, but she's got a killer body.

"Who are these people?" she asks, but then— "Aspen Davis?"

Aspen, who's already standing, says simply, "In the flesh."

Taylor gulps on the couch.

Hell, she should do more than gulp. She's seen what they did to Aspen.

"Margo..." Taylor begins.

"What the hell are you doing here? We thought you were dead." This from the wife.

"Apparently I'm not. What's up with the name change, Margo? Or Nancy?"

No response from either Taylor or her wife. Taylor, who

pretended she couldn't even remember this woman...and now we find out she's married to her? Something is wrong between this woman's ears. Taylor did say she wanted to protect Nancy...but to deny her?

"Listen," I say, "you have information we want."

"I feel like I'm looking at a ghost," Nancy says.

"You're not." From Aspen. "I'm as alive as you are. But Gloria? She's not. And I'm here to find out why."

"Gloria's dead?" Nancy's eyes widen.

"She is," I say. "Most likely because of something she knew. And I'm thinking maybe you have a little more knowledge than you're letting on."

"I don't know what you're—"

Taylor cuts Nancy off. "Save it. I'm so sorry. But they know."

"Know what? What are you talking about, Taylor?"

"For God's sake." I rub my forehead against the headache that's threatening to emerge. "Start talking."

I think about pulling my gun out of my ankle holster. That might get them talking.

But damn, I don't want to be that guy.

Aspen apparently doesn't have that problem.

She takes her shirt off again, pulls the gun out of its holster, and holds it on Taylor.

Start talking," she says.

I open my mouth to say something, but then I close it. Aspen has already made the move, and I can't stop her now.

"I'm not leaving without finding out who was behind what happened to me," Aspen says. "And you know what? You've seen what I look like now, Taylor. And Nancy, take a freaking look. I'd take my bra off so you can see my further disfigurement, but I'll let you use your imagination. You can call the cops on me if you want. But Buck over there? He's armed as well. He's an ex-Navy SEAL."

"Even ex-Navy SEALs aren't allowed to hold guns on people," Nancy says. "It's against the law."

"Is it?" Aspen drops her mouth into an O. "And all this time I thought it was only a crime to arrange for the abduction of people."

"What are you—"

"The two of you sold me into slavery," Aspen says.

They both turn white. Did they *really* not know what they were doing?

"We know that you know how it happened," I say. "So start talking."

"We can't." Taylor says. "They'll kill us."

"Oh? And who are *they*?"

"There's this guy. He..."

"He what?" From Aspen.

"He... "

"Taylor," Nancy says, "you've got to shut up."

"No," Taylor says. "I'm not going to shut up. I can't. I'm sorry. I can't save you, but I can save myself."

"You conniving little bitch."

"All right," I say. "We're not interested in a lover's spat. All we're interested in is the truth."

"Right," Aspen agrees. "Who the hell is this guy you're talking about?"

"Oh my God," I shake my head.

"What?"

"Taylor Wallace. Wallace Leathers."

"Yeah? Except no longer. He fucking disowned me."

"Gregory Simpson Wallace."

"That's my uncle," Taylor says.

"Right. I don't know why I didn't put two and two together."

"The business belongs to my father," Taylor says. "His name is Harrison Wallace."

"I understand. But Greg Wallace... He's on the list."

"What list?" Aspen asks.

"The list, Aspen," I say. "Of the men. The men who visited the island."

Aspen's jaw drops, and her complexion... I'm sure I'm imagining it, but she looks...green.

She's wondering... She's wondering if the uncle of the woman sitting next to her is responsible for any of her scarring. Physical or emotional.

"Where's your uncle now?" Aspen demands.

Taylor gulps. "In prison."

"Good. And your father?"

"My father didn't—"

"That's not what I mean," Aspen says. "Why the hell did your father disown you?"

Radio silence from Taylor.

"We're going to have to tell her," Nancy says. "Because if I'm going down, Taylor, you're going down with me."

20

ASPEN

I'm still holding my gun. I've been hoping Buck would bring his out, but he hasn't.

I kind of understand why.

I probably shouldn't have pulled mine out, but I did, so it's too late to back down now.

Plus, it gave me a chance to take off my shirt and force Nancy to look at my scars as well.

These two...

Whatever they have between them, it's not love. Why the hell are they even together?

Fucking Taylor bursts into tears again.

Nancy seems to be a little stronger. Icy, even. "I suppose it was bound to happen," she says.

Buck frowns. "Gee, and you went to all the trouble to change your name and everything."

Nancy twists her lips. "I don't suppose it would matter to you if I told you there isn't a day that I don't regret what we did?"

I scoff. "Absolutely right. It doesn't matter to me."

"Who killed Gloria?" This from Buck.

Nancy shakes her head. "Neither of us had anything to do with that."

"For God's sake, Nancy. Tell them the fucking truth. We didn't do the deed."

"Right." A slight shudder racks through Nancy. "But we know who did. And we didn't... We didn't think they'd be killed!"

"Who?" Buck demands.

And this time he brings out his gun.

He points it at Nancy, and she gets noticeably more nervous now that there's a gun at *her* head.

"A guy."

Buck holds the gun firm on Nancy. "I'm afraid we're going to need you to be a little more specific."

"He goes by Chris Pollack, but that's not his real name."

"Ice Man," I say, my voice low.

"Ice Man?" Taylor's voice shakes.

"One of the men who went to the island. He tormented a friend of mine. And now you're saying he's the one who killed Gloria?"

"Most likely the one who sent me to the hospital as well," Buck says.

"Some people," I say, "just can't leave well enough alone."

"Tell me why we shouldn't shoot both of you in the head right now," Buck says.

"I'm going to throw up," Taylor says.

"Are you?" I say. "Let me tell you all the times I threw up on that island. After having unthinkable things done to me. Things that resulted in these scars. A degenerate bit my nipple off, Nancy. Shattered my leg so I'll never jump again. So you can have your fucking position. I can no longer jump.

And some of those things? They may not show on the outside, but they scarred me the most horrifically."

"I'm so sorry." Taylor covers her face with her hands. "It was all Nancy's idea!"

"Seriously, bitch?" From Nancy.

My jaw drops. So much for this so-called marriage. This is more than a lovers' spat. "What the hell happened to you?" I ask Nancy. "I remember you being a nice person."

"Yeah? You came in out of nowhere and took the spot that was meant for Gloria. You bumped me down to third place. Guess I'm a damned good actress."

"My God..." I force my arm—I'm still holding my piece—to remain steady.

"I have to go to the bathroom." Taylor's hand goes over her mouth.

"You're not going anywhere," I say.

"Please... I'm going to be sick..."

I rise. "Fine. I'll go with you."

I follow her as she walks down a small hallway to a bathroom.

I keep the gun trained on Taylor. "I guess I can watch you throw up."

"No. Please..." She points to the small window above the bathtub. "There's no way I could get out that window."

"Somehow I think you'll find a way."

"Believe me. I can't. It doesn't even open."

Fine," I huff. "Empty your stomach and then get the hell back out here."

I leave her alone, and then I listen intently, my ear to the door.

I expect to hear retching sounds when—

I jerk when a gunshot rings out.

I toss the door open.

Taylor is slumped over the toilet, blood everywhere, and her brains are splattered onto the wall and floor of the bathroom.

I throw up in the sink.

I don't even feel the nausea, it just overtakes me, and I retch.

Buck comes running in, dragging Nancy with him.

"What the fuck?"

"She must've had a gun in here," I say, swallowing back another heave.

"Oh, baby. Are you all right?"

"No. Buck. I am so far from all right." I grip the edge of the sink with my left hand, the gun still in my right but pointed at the floor.

"This looks pretty good to me," Nancy says. "The two of you holding guns in my home. And now my wife's dead? Should be easy to convince someone that you killed her."

I turn and regard Nancy—who I thought, all those years ago, was a nice person. This is her reaction? To her wife, dead by her own hand? To her bathroom drenched in the brains and skull fragments of the woman she supposedly loves?

Nancy Mosely is a sociopath.

Nausea creeps up on me again.

"Get a grip," Buck says to Nancy. "Forensics will come out and will determine that first, the bullet came from Taylor's gun, not one of ours, and second, they'll determine that she died by her own hand based on the angles by which she was shot and the bullet trajectory."

Nancy's countenance is stoic, her facial features nearly without expression. "Maybe, but we have an eyewitness—me—who will say one of you killed her. With her own gun."

"Yeah," Buck says. "An eyewitness who changed her name. Who we'll be able to prove had something to do with Aspen's abduction. It won't work, Nancy. It's over."

"It's not over until I say it's over." Nancy turns.

Buck grabs her. "We're not going to shoot you. We won't become who you are."

"That's smart," she says, "because if you shoot me, no one will be able to lead you to Gloria's killer."

"Yeah, we're smart enough to know that too. But the first thing we need to do here is get the rest of your story."

"What if I don't feel like talking?"

"There are a lot of ways we can make you talk," I say. "As you can probably see by my body, I'm well-versed in the art of torture."

21

BUCK

Aspen doesn't quake. She doesn't flinch. In fact, she raises her arm once more, holds the gun on Nancy.

"Aspen..."I say.

"Why the hell not?" Aspen demands. "Look at me, Buck. I'm still not exactly sure what she did, but it was enough to make her wife kill herself rather than face the music. Shouldn't she endure something of what I endured?"

"Then you become no better than the people who held you captive."

"Maybe I *am* no better than they are."

I feign a sigh. "All right. You've convinced me. We'll torture her until she talks."

A frightened gasp comes out of Nancy.

I'm bluffing, of course, but it's important that neither Aspen nor Nancy understand that I am.

Aspen looks at me with a question in her eyes. Maybe she knows I'm bluffing.

Mostly likely. She knows I'm a SEAL. We don't torture.

Just like I know her. She may talk a good game, but when

push comes to shove? She won't be able to torture another human being.

She doesn't have it in her.

This is a woman who couldn't leave a dog to go to a shelter.

Nancy is far from an innocent dog, but Aspen still won't be able to do it.

And even if she can? I won't let her.

"Maybe we'll start with a few cuts," I say. "What kind of knives do you have in the kitchen, Nancy?"

"Please..."

"*Please*," Aspen echoes. "I stopped saying please on the island. It didn't do any good. But I said it a lot when I first got there. I pleaded. I begged. I promised to do anything they wanted if only they would stop hurting me. You know what? Please means nothing to me."

"You have to believe me. We didn't know what they had in mind for you."

"That doesn't really sway me. Sorry."

"Just talk," I say. "Talk, and you won't ever have to know what Aspen went through."

She gulps.

"Taylor said she had to protect you," Aspen says. "Is that why she killed herself?"

Nancy scoffs. "Taylor offed herself to save her own ass. She wasn't protecting me."

"Well, she's gone now, so no one is protecting you. You just sold yourself out." Aspen's voice never wavers.

"All right," she says. "But you should know that there *are* consequences to me talking."

"Do I look like I care?" Aspen says.

"No." Nancy shakes her head. "I don't think you care

about a goddamned thing, Aspen. There's a dead woman in my bathroom, and you don't seem to care."

"Funny," Aspen says. "This is the second time I've seen death. Each instance gets a little easier."

God, how her words ring true. And she has never even caused the death herself.

Each time, out in the field—each time it got easier to see a man bleed out. To see the rage of death on humanity.

Even when Amira was killed…

I never saw her body, thank God, but I could picture it in my mind. Though I loved her—though I would've done anything to have her back for one more moment so I could confess my feelings to her—the image in my mind of her exploded body made me less nauseated than the first time I saw death.

It does get easier.

It shouldn't, but it does.

"Your wife is gone," I say. "I'd say I'm sorry for your loss, but I'm not. I'm not convinced you are either. And if she had anything to do with putting Aspen on that island, then she got what was coming to her."

"It wasn't her idea," Nancy says.

"Whose was it, then?"

"It was her contact. Her uncle. Her Uncle Greg."

"Yeah, I figured that one out already. When I remembered the name and cross-referenced it."

"Why did you change your name?" Aspen asks. "Why didn't Taylor?"

"I just did what they told me to do."

"Who the fuck are *they*?" I demand.

My phone rings then.

Fuck. It's Raven.

I nod to Aspen. "I need to take this. You okay here?"

"I can get her to talk."

That's what I was afraid of, but I have to trust Aspen. Trust that she's a good human being with a good heart, and I know she is.

I nod back to her, and then I walk outside the house to take the call.

"Moreno," I say.

"It's me. I have news. We found Chris Pollack."

"Good. I have news too. Apparently he's the one who killed Gloria Delgado and Brian Hansen."

"Yeah, I was about to tell you the same thing. We found him, and he's talking."

"Why is he talking?"

"Let's just say he was convinced."

"Jesus Christ, Raven."

"Luke."

"No, Raven. If you're resorting to what I think you are, then you're still Raven."

"No, I'm Luke. It wasn't me who convinced him to talk. It was Katelyn."

22

ASPEN

Something rustles.

I'm not alone here.

I'm never alone here.

Then it's more than rustling.

Footsteps. Running footsteps.

Coming closer, coming—

I run. Thank God I'm fully hydrated because I need to run fast.

Whoever it is, he's gaining on me, and I understand now why Diamond gave me the shoes.

At least I can run, at least I can—

"I've got you, bitch. I see you!"

The voice is low, but the person is panting. Breathing hard.

I'm giving him a good chase.

Which is exactly what he wants.

What would happen if I stopped?

Stopped in my tracks and refused to run?

I won't.

I never do, but what if I did?

Would the thrill of the hunt be dead in him?

It's tempting, but it's not who I am.

I go. I move. I push myself to the limit, and then I find more within me, and I push harder.

That's what you do as an athlete.

That's what you do as an—

"Got you!"

I'm forced to the ground, and something snags my back as I fall.

"Ouch!" I cry out.

"It's true what they say about you." The voice comes from above me. "You're hard to catch. But I knew I could do it. I knew you couldn't outrun me."

I force my eyes to open. Above me stands a man, a huge man, wearing a white cotton mask over his entire face.

White, of course, because it reflects heat on this tropical island. Some of them wear black masks, and they must be hotter than hell.

His eyes are light blue. His body a pasty white. Almost too white.

Pasty white but ripped.

He wears only athletic shorts and a tank top, also white.

And running shoes of course. I can't see his feet from this angle, but I know he's wearing running shoes.

The only reason Diamond would've given me running shoes was because he asked her to.

He wanted me to be able to run.

He wanted me to be able to run so he could catch me.

"Let me go," I say through clenched teeth.

"Now why would I do that?"

"I made it too easy for you," I say. "I can run faster. Harder. And I bet you can't catch me."

"That's where you're wrong, bitch. I will always catch you."

"Will you?"

"I got you this time, didn't I?"

"You did, but now I know who you are. I've been able to assess you, and I can adapt."

He laughs then. A satanic guttural laugh. If I didn't know better, I'd think I were staring at the devil himself.

The devil in a white mask.

Is the devil a red-eyed demon? A serpent?

Not here. Not on this island.

The devil takes many forms here.

"Fine, you little bitch. Run. I'll even give you a five minute start. And I will fucking catch you. And when I do? I'm going to fuck you. I'm going to fuck you hard."

Does he think that's supposed to scare me? I've been raped more times than I can count. I've been bitten, beaten, stabbed. Sent to the infirmary even.

This tyrant doesn't scare me.

This tyrant is a fucking challenge.

"Is that what you want? To fuck me? Then why not do it right now?"

His guttural satanic laugh again.

This time it reverberates through my body and into the ground beneath me. I can almost feel the earth shake.

"It's all the sweeter when I catch you."

*"But you've already caught me...*sir.*"*

*Yes, I give a snide emphasis to "*sir*" because it will piss him off. And that's what I'm counting on.*

"I could, you know," he says. "I could slide my hard dick into that cunt right now. I could fuck you so hard you'd bleed."

"Then what's stopping you?"

He growls then. He sounds like a fucking lion standing over its prey.

But then he moves off of me. He stands.

"Get up," he says, his voice a rasp.

I don't.

I lie there.

And I know I'm in for something that will change my life.

I'M STILL HOLDING the gun on Nancy.

I don't know how long Buck will be gone talking to Luke. In the meantime, it takes every ounce of strength I possess not to pistol-whip this bitch.

"Talk," I say.

"Don't you want to wait until he gets back?"

"I've waited long enough, don't you think?"

"You've only been here a—"

"That's not what I'm talking about, you maniac. I'm talking about the five years I spent on that damned island being hunted. Tortured. Raped. So yeah, I've waited long enough."

She sighs. "We didn't realize—"

"Save it. You wanted to get rid of me, and you did. Do you think I care whether you realized at the time what would happen to me? I don't. You stole five years of my life just because you wanted Gloria to be in my position so you could be her second. Second! You sold a fellow human being down the river for fucking *second*! None of this even makes sense to me. Was there money? Prestige? Or are you just a sociopath?"

She doesn't reply. Not that I expect her to.

Finally, Buck returns. "Aspen, we have to go."

"What do we do with her?" I'm still pointing my gun at Nancy.

"We take her with us." Buck says.

"Where? Where are we going?"

"To a safe house. Near Katelyn's place."

"A safe house?"

"Luke has...connections."

Right. Connections. From his drug lord past.

"I don't like the idea any more than you do," Buck continues, "but he's got Pollack there."

Nancy's eyes widen, and she gasps. "No, don't take me there."

"Listen. I don't have a clue why my position was so important to you," Aspen says.

"Come on," Nancy scoffs.

"You weren't even going to get it," I say. "It was going to go to Gloria, not you."

"I have my reasons."

"Well, I don't give a rat's ass what they were. You put me through hell."

"I—"

"Save it. When I say hell, I mean literal Hell, Nancy. You can't even imagine what happened to me on that island."

"I'm not blind, Aspen. I can see the scars."

"Seeing the scars and having them inflicted on you is not the same thing at all."

Nancy stays quiet then.

Until—

"You have to believe me. Please. We had no idea this is what would happen to you."

"What did you think would happen to me?"

"You were going to be out of the way."

"Are you that naïve? What do you think out-of-the-way means?"

She gulps. "I guess I didn't think that far."

Buck intervenes then. "That's bullshit, and you and I both know it. Maybe you didn't imagine that she would be taken to an island and hunted like an animal, but you knew that out-of-the-way did not mean anything good."

Nancy stays silent.

"Let's go," Buck says. "The sooner we figure this out and get to the bottom of this, the sooner you can move on with your life, baby."

23

BUCK

My phone rings then. It's a number I don't recognize. But I better take it. Who knows who could be calling me with relevant information right now?

"Moreno," I say to the phone.

"Buck, Darnell Davis."

Aspen's father? Maybe he's just calling to check in on Aspen. Did I give him my number? Perhaps Aspen did.

"Yes, hello."

"Can you speak freely?"

"Of course."

"Is Aspen with you?"

"Yes," I say hesitantly.

"Move to a location where she can't overhear what you're saying," Darnell says.

Uh-oh.

This can't be good.

"Give me a second." I mute the phone call. "I need to take this outside. Keep your eye on Nancy."

Aspen opens her mouth to object, but I leave the room quickly and stand outside the front door.

"All right, Darnell. I'm alone."

"Good. I found a connection."

"We found a connection as well," I say. "A couple girls on the volleyball team who wanted Aspen out of the way."

"Interesting. Does it by any chance have anything to do with a man named Greg Wallace?"

I nearly drop my phone, but I catch it in time. "Actually… it does. What are you trying to tell me, Darnell?"

"Greg Wallace is the brother of Harrison Wallace, of Wallace Leathers. The leather king."

"I know that," I say. "Though I didn't know he was called the leather king."

"It's what he calls himself. Sounds like an idiot, but he's not the issue. You probably know that Taylor Wallace, his daughter, was one of Aspen's teammates."

"Yes, and she's dead."

"What the hell do you mean she's dead? I just had my guys checking her out!"

"Well she's been dead for all of a half-hour. She offed herself when we confronted her."

"For fuck's sake. She has information."

"She *did*, and we got most of it out of her. Plus her wife, Nancy Mosely, is still alive, and she seems to have more information."

"Do not let that woman kill herself," Darnell says.

"We won't. Aspen's got her at gunpoint right now."

"What the fuck are you saying to me?" Darnell grits out. "Why are you letting my baby tree hold a gun?"

"Do you know your daughter, sir? Nobody *lets* her do anything."

Darnell pauses a moment. "I taught her how to handle firearms myself. The girl's a natural."

"She is. We went to a shooting range, and she knows her stuff." I clear my throat. "So what's the connection between you and Greg Wallace?"

"He served underneath me in Desert Shield. I got him kicked out of the Navy."

"Okay. But I'm not sure how I see the connection."

"Greg Wallace went to that island." Darnell says.

"Yeah, I know that. His name's on the list."

"I only just got the list this morning. Called in a few favors."

"Hell, I could've given you the list."

"I didn't know you had it."

"I do, and you're right. Gregory Simpson Wallace is on the list. Do you think he had a grudge against you, and he took it out on your daughter?"

"Yeah, I think that's it. Aspen happened to be in the wrong place at the wrong time, and once Wallace found out she was mine..." Heavy breathing on the other end of the line. "I'm not sure I can ever forgive myself. Lisa can't know about this. She'll never forgive me either."

"Listen, Darnell. This wasn't your fault. Greg Wallace is a psycho. Obviously you know that, because you got him kicked out of the SEALs."

"For sure that's true. He was a hothead. Quick to pull a trigger. No place for him in the SEALs or in any military outfit."

"So it was a dishonorable discharge then?"

"It was. I can give you the details, but it's a long story."

"I trust you. I'll get the story another time. But Darnell,

right now, we need to take down anyone who had anything to do with this."

"Greg Wallace is in prison," Darnell says. "Although that's too damned good for him."

"I agree, but you and I are sane and rational people. We're not vigilantes."

"I don't know, Moreno," Darnell says. "I'm feeling pretty vigilante right now."

I'm not surprised. The apple doesn't fall far from the tree. Aspen is ready to go vigilante herself.

But I have to protect her.

I have to protect her from what will happen to her if she does attempt to make her own justice. She and her father are both sane individuals. Good strong people. But damn, they both have a hot streak.

"Listen," I tell Darnell. "Someone I know is holding a man named Chris Pollack, who was also part of this. Aspen and I are going to go question him, and we're going to take Nancy Mosely with us."

"The wife?"

"Right."

"What the hell are you going to do about the dead body?"

Damn. I hadn't thought of that. "I guess we'll call 911 and let them find her. It's clear she offed herself. Plus she used her own gun."

"Good, good." Darnell says.

"All right. Thank you for the information and I—"

"Wait just a minute. Are you dismissing me, Moreno?"

"No, of course not."

Aspen doesn't want her father involved. What do I do?

"Good. Let me know where you're holding this guy, and I'll come to you."

"Darnell..."

"You think I'm some old man who can't handle himself?"

"Of course not. It's not me. It's Aspen. She doesn't want you involved. She's protecting you."

"It's not her job to protect me. It's my job to protect her, and I've failed miserably. She's my daughter. My baby tree. And I *will* be involved in this."

"What about Lisa?"

He pauses again.

"Lisa will understand," he finally says. "She always does."

I want to stop him. I want to talk him out of this. But how? He feels responsible now. There's a link to him that may have started all of this.

All he wants is to protect his little girl.

He wants the same thing I want.

And he feels like he failed.

God, I get that. I failed to protect Emily from Lucifer Raven. I failed to protect Amira.

I *won't* fail again.

I sigh. "All right, Darnell." I give him the address of the safe house, and I hope like hell Lucifer Raven—Luke—won't be pissed.

But if he is? Oh well.

I'm more concerned with Aspen's wrath.

She's going to be mad as hell that I brought her father into this.

"I can get there in an hour," Darnell says.

"Wait. You're in LA?"

"Yep. Just got here. As soon as I figured out this connection, I got in my truck and started driving."

"All right. An hour. That's about the time we'll be arriving.

Wait outside until we get there. And we'll do the same if we get there first. We need to go in together."

"My little tree is with you?"

"She is, Darnell. And she's no longer a little tree. She's a mighty fucking oak. You'd be proud of her."

"I always was, Moreno. I still am. And I will take down the people who did this to my little tree if it's the last thing I do."

24

ASPEN

Buck drives, and Nancy and I sit in the backseat. I press my gun firmly into her side the whole time.

To say I don't trust her is an understatement.

This conniving bitch...

"Why all of this?" I ask her. "You're a software engineer, for God's sake. Why did you even play pro volleyball?"

"Because I was good at it."

"You were third choice," I say. "Granted, that's a hell of a lot better than most, but you had a degree in engineering. The sky's the limit. Especially for women in the field."

"I love volleyball," she says simply.

Does it truly come down to that? Hell, I loved volleyball too. In some ways, I still do, but I know I'll never play the sport again. First of all, I physically can't. Not after the bone fractures I suffered on the island. But that's not the issue. The issue is the nerve damage that came along with the bone fractures.

Damn, that day on the island.

When all I had was a pair of running shoes.

I put up a damned good fight—in my mind, at least—but I ultimately lost.

"GET UP," Pasty Guy grits out.

"No."

"I said get up, you bitch."

Why should I give him what he wants? He'll find me anyway. He will eventually hunt me down, do what he wants to me. He's already caught me. Why the hell does he want me to run again?

It's the thrill of the chase.

But he already caught me, so I'm a little confused.

And I don't fucking care. He's going to do what he's going to do.

"Get up and run," he says again, "or you'll wish you had."

My breathing has finally returned to normal. I could get up. I have renewed energy, and endorphins are coursing through me. I could get up, and I could run.

But that would be doing what he wants.

"They told me you were worth it," he says. "They told me you were a challenge. So far? You're nothing more than the rest of them."

This is a man who gets off on a challenge. He may be pasty white and disgusting, but he is all muscle.

"Get the fuck up, and make me work for it, bitch. Show me what you've got."

But I don't want to give him what he wants. This is the only fight I have in me. He wants me to run? If I do what he demands, I'm acquiescing.

I'm so tired *of acquiescing.*

I'm a fighter. I want to fight. With everything inside me, I want to rise and run like hell. But that's what he wants.

I have to go against my instincts now.

I have to refuse to fight.

"No," I say.

His fist meets my cheek in a dull punch. A sharp pain at first, and then a dull ache. That's how it always happens. The pain is so intense you think you may die at first, but then...just a simple ache.

"There'll be more of that if you don't get up and run."

There will be more of that anyway. I've been here a while. I know the drill. Does he think I'm stupid?

"I'll put you in the fucking hospital," he says.

He'll probably do that anyway. Is that supposed to scare me?

I repeat my thoughts. "Is that supposed to scare me?"

"Sure as hell should, bitch."

"Why? Do you think there's anything you can do to me that someone else already hasn't? I doubt your ideas are that unique."

"You'd be surprised."

I wince as another blow comes to my head. First the sharp pain, and within seconds, the ache. I can live with the ache. I kind of always ache now.

A ring of light crosses the path of my vision.

Nothing new there. A blow to the head does that to me. I found that out on the volleyball court one time when I was hit on the head by a ball and it knocked me off balance. Then I hit my head on the floor of the court.

Ring of light city.

"Get up," Pasty Guy says again, his voice lower this time.

Rage radiates from him. I can almost see it turning the ring of light red around me.

Pasty white he may be. Masked he may be. But he is still the devil.

I could get up.

I could rise and run with renewed energy. It would be easy.

But I don't. I lie there.

"I can make you get up," he says. "I can bring people in here to force you to stand up."

"Do it. You know what that means? It means you can't handle me alone." It takes effort but I hock a wad of saliva and spit it in his face.

A blow to my head, and then another.

I lose consciousness.

And it's a good thing I do, because later, when I wake up?

I wish I were dead.

"YOU OKAY, ASPEN?" Buck's voice from the front seat.

"Yeah. Fine." I clear my throat.

"You got quiet back there."

"I don't have anything to say to this bitch."

"That's all right," Buck says. "We'll get the whole story soon enough."

He pulls up to a remote area in the desert. A small shack stands there.

And then—

I gasp. My father. My father's truck.

"Buck, what did you do?"

"I didn't do anything, baby. He's here of his own volition."

"How did he know to come here?"

Buck doesn't answer.

Knots tangle in my stomach. I'm both fearful and angry. Angry at Buck for bringing my father into this, and fear for both of them. "How could you?" I say.

No response from Buck. He simply pulls the car as close

as he can, turns off the engine, gets out, and opens the back door, pulling Nancy out.

I scramble out the other side while my father leaves his vehicle.

I want to run to him. I want to beg him to go away. But I can't. I don't want to make any noise, because I don't know what waits for us inside that little house.

"Captain," Buck says.

"Moreno." From my father.

He's wearing fatigues and army boots. Buck is wearing jeans and army boots.

I'm wearing shorts and running shoes.

Running shoes…

They sure as hell didn't save me that day, but maybe they'll save me today.

"Little tree," Dad says, "Moreno and I are going in. You and whoever that is stay out here. Keep your gun on her."

"I'm going in, Dad."

"Your father's right," Buck says. "Let us go in first."

"I'm not some soft woman you have to coddle."

"We know that, little tree. Still, I'm your father. It's my job to protect you. I failed you in the past, but I will do it today."

I sigh. "All right, Daddy. Please… Please stay safe. Keep Buck safe. And yourself," I turn to Buck. "Don't you dare let anything happen to my father. Or yourself."

25

BUCK

I knock hesitantly on the door.

"Moreno?" Luke's voice.

"Yeah, it's me."

A click of the lock, and then the door opens.

Luke stands there, dressed in all black. He looks at Darnell. "Who the hell is this?"

"Aspen's father."

"What's he doing here?"

"You can speak directly to me," Darnell says, his voice low. "This concerns me as much as it does the rest of you. She's my little girl."

"He's good." I say to Luke. "He's a former SEAL, like I am."

"Which is more than you are," Darnell says. "Being an ex-criminal."

"Emphasis on the *ex*," Luke says.

"I use the *ex* only out of respect for what you've done for my daughter. Once a criminal, always a criminal in my book."

Jesus Christ. Darnell's not helping himself, though I can't fault his logic. I don't like Luke either.

"Forget it," Luke says. "There's nothing we can do about it now. You know why we're here. Get in here."

I go in first, followed by Darnell.

"Aspen's outside with Nancy Mosely," I tell Luke.

"Okay. Good enough. I've got Pollack here."

"Where's Katelyn?"

"She's back at the beach house, under constant guard."

"I thought you said she's the one who got him to talk."

"She did. Via a secure channel on the phone. I wouldn't bring her here." He looks me over.

Is he fucking judging me? For bringing Aspen here? What the hell choice did I have?

"I don't like that look you're giving me."

"I don't like it either." From Darnell.

"Look, you don't have to like it. I don't have to like either of you. We're all here for the same reason: to bring these motherfuckers down."

I guess I have no argument there. Neither does Darnell, apparently.

"Follow me," Luke says.

We go into a back room.

A man sits tied to a wooden chair, his mouth covered in duct tape. He's an older guy, nothing remarkable about him except for...

His eyes. They're such a light brown that they're almost yellowish.

"That's Pollack?" I say.

"The one and only," Luke says. "Or Ice Man, as Katelyn calls him."

"Why does she call him that?"

"Trust me," Luke says. "You don't want to know."

Chris Pollack is a middle-aged man, grayish and balding.

From his build I can tell he was once muscular, but now? He's let himself go.

Both of his eyes are bruised, most likely from Luke. Bummer. I would've liked to do it myself.

"This is the man who killed Gloria Delgado and Brian Hansen," Luke says. "He admitted it."

I walk up to him and force myself not to clock him in his smug little head. "You fucking son of a bitch."

Pollack says nothing, of course. His mouth is strapped with duct tape. But he does flinch slightly.

Good.

"So what's his connection to Greg Wallace?" I ask.

"He's the one who ratted him out," Luke says.

"Right," I say. "That's why you're walking around as a free man, isn't it, Ice Man? You turned canary on your friends."

Pollack grunts against the duct tape.

"Yeah," Luke says. "Apparently, he negotiated his freedom by turning over several of the men who went to the island. That's why Wallace is in jail. He didn't have enough money to buy his own damned freedom."

"And neither did you, huh, Pollack?" I say. "You bought yours on the hides of your friends."

He grunts against the tape again.

I walk toward him and rip it off, hoping it hurts like hell.

He coughs and sputters.

"Start talking."

Darnell pulls out the Glock that he's holding at his side. "That's right. Start talking."

"Already told him everything." Pollack glances at Luke.

"We want to hear it again," I say.

"And we want to hear it now." From Darnell.

"I—"

Darnell hits him over the head with his pistol. "Let me make one thing clear. That little girl out there? Aspen Davis? She's my daughter. I don't know if you did anything to her on that island, and I don't really care. I'm going to see you to your grave anyway. But not until you talk."

"Why should I talk to you if you're going to kill me anyway?"

"Because I might make you suffer a little less if you cooperate."

I get what Darnell's doing. Apparently Pollack already told Luke everything, but Darnell is full of rage, full of the need for revenge. Just like his daughter is.

"I never touched her on that island," Pollack says.

"But others did."

"Yes," Pollack gulps out.

"Katelyn was his favorite," Luke says dryly. "And believe me, I *want* you to make him suffer."

Darnell gets a glaring and vengeful look in his brown eyes.

Damn, the guy means business.

He's a SEAL. A decorated SEAL.

But this is his daughter.

His daughter who is my everything.

I understand.

But I also don't think he's going to do anything. He's just making Pollack think he will.

"Guys came to me. Your men," he says to Luke.

"Not my men. Not any longer."

"Well, they were still your men."

"Did I force you to get in bed with the drug lords of LA? No, but you did it anyway. You did it because of me. Because of Katelyn. You got in with some bad folks, Ice Man."

"Keep talking," Darnell says.

"Your men," he says to Luke again. "Your men turned me over. Turned me over to a cabal, a prison underground. To Greg Wallace."

"So this Greg Wallace is some bigwig in prison?"

"Not really. He just used all the leverage he had for this favor."

"And what favor would that be?" I ask.

"He needed two people taken care of. Gloria Delgado and her husband. Seems they had been asking questions, or people had been asking them questions, about another one of the women from the island. Your daughter," he says to Darnell.

"And?" Darnell says between clenched teeth.

"Wallace said I owed him. He was behind bars because of me, and the drug lords turned me over to him."

"What could he do to you behind bars?" Darnell asks.

"Surely you're not that ignorant," Pollack says.

Darnell hits him in the head with the pistol again. "I'm not ignorant at all, asshole. But I want you to spell it out for me anyway. I want to hear it from your fucking mouth."

"Tell them," Luke says. "You're such an idiot, Pollack. You got immunity. You could've gotten away from all this, but once you saw Katelyn, you couldn't. Obsession runs deep."

Luke's eyes reflect knowledge. He understands obsession. He was once obsessed with my sister. Anger makes my neck grow hot, but I suppress it. I can't go there right now.

"How many times am I going to have to repeat myself?" Pollack demands.

"As many as I say." Darnell clocks him on his head once more. "Or I'll put you out like a light, and then we'll have to wait here until you wake up and can start talking again. That will make us angry, dumbass. And then we'll make it a lot worse for you."

"Fine, fine!" Pollack gasps, sweat trickling from his forehead. "I'll talk."

Darnell moves back a few steps. "I'm listening."

"I didn't know Greg's connection to Aspen. Not until recently. Greg and I saw each other on the island a couple of times. But you know, it was a gentlemen's deal."

I scoff. "A gentlemen's deal? You guys think you are actually *gentlemen*?"

"You know what I mean. Don't ask, don't tell, and all that. Anything we saw on the island was always in confidence. We signed a document to that effect."

"Until you could buy your freedom for that information," I say. "Then your so-called gentlemen's deal meant nothing."

He doesn't respond.

"Keep talking." From Darnell.

"We knew each other from the island. I was told, when I made my immunity deal, that none of the information would ever be made public. That no one would know I had given the names."

"Yeah," Luke says, "that was before you immersed yourself into my previous world."

Pollack chokes a little. "Could you loosen these bindings around my chest? I'm feeling really tight. Like I can't breathe."

"No," Luke says flatly.

"Please. I think I might be having a heart attack."

I look at him. There's no sweat on his face other than what's already emerged at his receding hairline. He's not breathing heavily.

"You're bluffing. Keep talking."

He winces a few times, but then he gives up the ruse. "The LA drug people found out all the names that I had given to the feds. Greg Wallace was one of them. Somehow that information got to Greg in prison."

I roll my eyes. "Yeah, I'm sure it did *somehow*."

"Anyway, your people"—he glances at Luke—"threatened me."

"They're no longer my people. Say it again and I'll let this angry father here cut you up into tiny little pieces."

"Please, no!" Pollack gasps. Then, "Greg found out that one of the people who knew of his involvement was talking to Aspen and you. He needed those people taken care of."

"So you're saying *you* killed Gloria and Brian?" I ask.

"I did," he gulps out.

"I don't buy it. It had to have been someone they knew. There was no sign of a struggle."

"I wasn't alone," Pollack says. "Someone else was with me. Someone they knew."

26

ASPEN

Shattered tibia and fibula.

Nerve damage.

Nerve damage.

Nerve damage.

Voices around me, and then Diamond.

"Garnet, can you hear me? Garnet?"

The sounds are coming through a funnel or something.

They make it to my ears, but there's something unreal about them. Maybe I'm underwater.

Maybe...

Did he drown me?

No.

They're not allowed to kill us.

There aren't any pools deep enough for them to hold us down and drown us, not on the hunting ground.

Still...

If I were drowning, would I be able to breathe?

Am I breathing?

I'm numb. So numb.

Can't move my leg.

My left leg.

There's a searing pain.

Searing pain all around my right breast.

"She's coming to." Not Diamond's voice.

An image emerges in my peripheral vision.

A woman. A woman in scrubs. Green scrubs.

"Garnet. Garnet, can you hear me?"

Yes.

But the words don't come out. Only a soft squeak.

"She's trying to talk," Green Scrubs says.

Then Diamond's face. Her kind and wrinkled face in my field of vision. She's blurry, but I recognize her.

She's the only person I recognize.

"Garnet, you're going to be here for a couple of months. It's a respite."

I try to open my mouth.

"It's okay. Don't try to talk. Your tibia and fibula on your left leg are broken. Shattered. You've got some damage to your right breast. But you will be fine. Your bones need to knit together. You've had surgery. It will take some time, but you will be good as new again."

Where am I? Is this person a doctor? Am I still on the island?

I lose consciousness then.

Maybe Diamond's right.

Enjoy the respite.

~

I'M SO TIRED. My arm hurts from holding the gun on Nancy.

But I never waver.

I learned one thing on that damned island, something

even more important than what my athletic training taught me.

Sometimes you have to run.

I don't know if I would've been worse off if I had done what the man asked. If I had run when he told me to run.

I was just so tired of being told what to do.

I knew he would eventually catch me because the odds were always in the man's favor.

And this man? He was as ripped a man as I'd ever seen. Made me wonder why he never wanted to get in the sun. Even a little bit of sun would've made him less pasty white. There was not an ounce of fat on him. He was all muscle.

So I fought. I fought by *not* giving him what he wanted.

And damn, I paid the price.

That's why I'll never play volleyball again.

I healed. It took several months and a lot of physical therapy, but I healed. Turned out the island had top notch medical care for all the women. Those physicians and therapists must have been well paid to keep quiet about what they saw. They had one job—to get us healed and back to work. After all, if I hadn't been able to heal and get back out on the hunt, I was nothing more than garbage to be thrown out.

So I was determined, and I healed. I got my strength back, I learned to run again, I kept my muscles in shape.

But I knew I would never again be a professional athlete.

I could run, but I could no longer jump.

I look down at my left leg, at the scars on my left calf from the halo device that kept my bones in place while they healed. Not all the scars are from the men on the island.

But they were the result of what I endured on the island.

"Can you just put the gun down, for a minute?" Nancy says.

"Absolutely not."

"Aren't you tired?"

Yes. "Absolutely not," I grit out.

"I didn't know. Please. You have to believe me. I didn't know."

I do believe her. She's a nasty-ass bitch, but I don't think she's truly evil. Or at least she wasn't then. Now? She's a certified sociopath.

"I don't believe you," I say.

"I just... It was a lot of things."

"Right."

"You just walked in, took the position from Gloria. Bumped me into third place."

"You were a setter, Nancy. You had a place. I've heard all this bullshit before." Then something dawns on me. "It was you and Taylor, wasn't it? You and Taylor were the two people that Gloria heard talking."

"Yeah."

"I knew she was lying. She told me she didn't recognize the voices, but she would've known Taylor's voice. They were dating."

"Gloria was a little screwed up," Nancy says. "And it was all because of you."

"Yeah, whatever. She couldn't stand the negative feelings she was having about me. Such a good little devout girl, who was having horrible feelings about the person who took her position away. Cry me a fucking river."

"It was more than that."

"Really? I don't care."

"She didn't stay on the team long after your disappearance. She felt a lot of guilt about it."

I roll my eyes. "Really? She told me she got injured. That's why she left the team."

"She did," Nancy says. "But she could have stayed on the team. She left. The guilt was killing her. The injury was just a convenient excuse to leave."

"The guilt, huh? From what I can tell she didn't have much to do with it."

"No, she didn't."

"That worked out well for you then. Once she left, that bumped you into the first position. You were the middle blocker."

Nancy doesn't reply.

She doesn't have to.

It's written all over her face.

"How do you live with yourself?" I ask. "I disappear. Then Gloria leaves the team, which I have a feeling you knew was going to happen. And now your wife is dead because of all of this."

Nancy scoffs. "Taylor and I weren't in love."

"Oh?"

"Taylor never really got over Gloria. And I'm not even gay."

I drop my jaw. "Then what the hell is all of this about?"

"It was best for us to stick together. It made sense, at least that's what we were told," Nancy says. "Taylor had already lost so much."

"But why did she lose her inheritance? How did her father even know what his brother was up to?"

"You'd have to ask Taylor that," Nancy says. "Oh wait. You can't. She's dead."

"If you know anything else, you'd better level with me." I

prod her with the gun in her side. "Because if you don't? My boyfriend and my father will see that you pay."

"A couple of Navy SEALs? I don't think so, Aspen. No Navy SEALs I know would ever harm a woman."

She's right of course. Neither my father nor Buck will harm her.

"Just how many Navy SEALs *do* you know?"

"Does it matter? Navy SEALs are honorable."

"You're right. Perhaps I misspoke." I dig the nose of the pistol into her side a tad harder. "Let me make this clear then. *I* will make sure you pay. Me. Aspen Davis, the woman you wronged. And I have absolutely no qualms about bringing harm to a woman whose actions contributed to my five years in hell."

27

BUCK

"Who was with you?" I ask.

"Who do you think? Taylor Wallace and her wife, Margo."

Margo. AKA Nancy Mosely. The woman Aspen is holding outside this very house.

And Taylor?

There's no way we can confront her since she chose to end her own life rather than face this music.

"Did they see what you did?" I ask.

"No. I didn't come in until later. They went by on the supposed social visit, and Gloria invited them in of course. They had to persuade her."

"What do you mean?" Darnell asks.

"Apparently they hadn't kept in touch, so Gloria thought it was kind of weird that they just showed up. But they made up some kind of excuse and Gloria eventually let them in. Then of course we had to get rid of that yappy little dog."

Good thing Aspen isn't here to hear this. She loves that pup.

"What did you do to the dog?" Darnell cocks his pistol.

"Hold your fire," Pollack says. "We just put him outside."

"You put him outside?"

"Well, later. After the sedative had taken effect."

"So what happened exactly?" I ask. "Taylor and Nancy go over, feign that they want to visit, Gloria invites them in, and..."

"They put a sedative in their drinks. The whole thing took about half an hour."

"All right, and then..."

"Then I went in. I moved them to their bed, let the dog out, and... I suppose you can guess the rest."

"And why are you admitting all of this?" From Darnell.

"I..."

Luke intervenes then. "It was Katelyn. She said some things to him..."

"What things?" My voice is low.

"Things she didn't mean of course. Things that made me puke. But it worked."

"So you have a soft spot for Katelyn," I say to Pollack.

"To me, she'll always be Moonstone."

"I don't even want to consider what you might've done to her," Darnell says. "You better have never touched my little girl."

"I didn't. Garnet's not my type."

Darnell grits his teeth, and his jaw goes even more rigid. For a moment I think he's going to pursue this. Demand to know why his little tree isn't this derelict's type.

Then he appears to think better of that.

Thank God.

"What do we do with him?" I ask.

"We turn him in," Luke says. "His immunity will be struck down. He'll go to prison."

I yank Luke aside for a minute. "What about *your* immunity?" I whisper. "You kidnapped a guy, tied him up, and held him at gunpoint. Surely that's enough criminal behavior to lose your deal."

"I'll worry about that," he whispers back.

"Look. It's not like I care. But Katelyn..."

"I said I'll take care of it." Luke goes rigid and walks back to Pollack. "Get ready for prison, asshole."

Fine, then. I'll file Luke's immunity issue under the heading of "not my problem."

"Looks like you'll be going to trial for two murders," Darnell says. "Plus the crimes you committed on that island."

"Whatever," Pollack says. "If I can't have Moonstone, life isn't worth living anyway."

"Oh, you'll live," Luke says. "And trust me, prison will be hell for you."

"Prison is hell for everyone," he says. "Why do you think I struck the deal in the first place?"

"You have no idea what hell is," Luke says. "You think Greg Wallace has connections in prison? You don't even want to know what *my* connections are. You'll wish you were dead."

"Maybe I'll just take my own life."

"They don't let you do that in prison, Pollack," Luke says. "They'll put you on suicide watch."

"That means I'll be well guarded, and in solitary."

"You'd think, wouldn't you?" Luke shakes his head, his blue eyes filled with smoke. "Lots of things can happen to a man in solitary. Especially if I happen to know the officers guarding you."

"You're going to go down with me. All three of you. False imprisonment is a crime as well."

"I don't think so," Darnell says. "Two former Navy SEALs, the father and the boyfriend of a woman who was tormented on that island? And a man with immunity? Who happens to be the fiancée of a woman from that island? Nobody will buy it."

"But it's the truth!" Pollack squawks.

"The truth is overrated," Luke says. "Believe me."

A FEW HOURS LATER, Chris Pollack is in custody, and Darnell, Luke, and I are free to go. Just like the old man predicted.

Also in custody is Nancy Mosely.

She tried like hell to squawk on Aspen, tried to get her on assault with a deadly weapon, but Aspen remained calm. Said she only did what she had to do to protect herself.

The intake officer was gutted by the story of her ordeal on the island, and that was all it took.

Aspen was also free.

Chris Pollack's arraignment is tomorrow, and we all have to be present. We won't have to testify at an arraignment, but the officers have requested that we be there.

Right now, though?

We can go.

I'm exhausted. I'm still recovering from my injuries, and today took a lot out of me.

I don't really want to stay at Luke's place, but his security is top-notch, and I want Aspen under constant guard, especially if she's a potential witness.

Pollack is now in custody, and Greg Wallace is in prison. Nancy is in custody and Taylor's dead.

Still… I won't take any chances with Aspen's life.

Darnell joins us at the beach house as well.

"I need to call Lisa," he says.

"I want to talk to Mom," Aspen says.

"All right, little tree. Come with me. Let's go outside and give her a call."

That leaves me with Luke and Katelyn.

I turn to Katelyn. "Hey, I'm sorry you had to talk to Ice Man, but thank you."

"It made my skin crawl," she admits, "but Aspen's life was in danger. And I know how much finding the truth means to her. And now… I hope she'll calm down. Try to truly heal."

"I hope so too," I say.

"And you don't have to worry about Ice Man ever again," Luke says. "He's going away for a long, long time. And believe me. Prison will be hell for him."

I almost expect Katelyn to tell Luke to go easy on him, but she doesn't.

Apparently she doesn't care if Pollack gets abused in prison. Why should she? He abused others. An eye for an eye and all.

Everything has turned out fine.

Except…

Something tingles at the back of my neck.

I don't think we're out of the woods yet. I can't say why, but it's just a hunch.

And one thing I learned in Afghanistan?

Never ignore a fucking hunch.

28

ASPEN

"I'm fine, Mom," I say into the phone.

Dad has the phone on speaker and we're talking to my mother.

Her voice is distraught, and she's been crying.

"Thank God you're both all right. Darnell, you get your ass home."

"I can't, honey. Not yet. I need to be at the arraignment tomorrow."

"Can't they do that without you?"

"No. I'm a material witness. This is a man who killed two people," Darnell says. "And also a man who violated Aspen's friend and countless others. He got off with immunity for turning on his friends. Not that I care about any of them, but this is not a good man, Lisa. I need to be here to see this through."

"Then I'm getting on a flight to LA," my mother says.

"No, Mom." I intervene this time. "I don't want you here. I didn't even want Dad here. You need to stay safe where you are. These people... They have connections. Big connections that we can't protect you from."

Mom gulps. I hear it through the phone.

"Lisa, precious," Dad says, "I will be home. As soon as this guy is arraigned and safely behind bars and the local PD has no more use for me."

"Is his immunity federal?" my mom asks.

"Most likely," Dad says. "I don't know all of the details. But he confessed to murdering two people in cold blood. Little tree and I and two others are witnesses. We have to be there."

She sighs. "All right. I understand. But I want you to get your butt back home as soon as you can."

"He will, Mom." I clear my throat. "In the meantime, Buck has arranged for a bodyguard for you."

Mom gasps through the phone.

"I okayed it, Lisa." Dad says. "It's important, honey. Don't fight me on this."

Another gulp through the line. "I won't. I won't, Darnell."

"Good. I love you."

"I love you too. Both of you."

"Love you too, Mom."

Dad ends the call.

"Now what?" I ask.

"I guess we join the others."

After a subdued dinner, I head to my bedroom.

I'd like to stay with Buck, but he needs his rest, and my father's under this roof.

It feels too weird.

I shower to get all the grime of the day off me. Has anyone even found Taylor's body yet?

What is the connection? Why did Taylor's father disown her?

Clearly it has something to do with this whole situation. He must've known about his brother. Or he knew about what Taylor did.

That's the connection. Taylor went to her uncle to get rid of me, and Taylor's dad found out and disinherited her.

But we'll never know for sure.

We'll never know because Taylor's dead.

Damn you Taylor. Damn you to hell.

My door creaks open.

I jerk toward it, but then I sigh.

Buck stands there.

He's freshly showered also, wearing a simple white T-shirt and blue lounging pants. His feet are bare, and his hair is wet.

He looks absolutely scrumptious.

"What are you doing in here?"

"I was hoping you'd come to my room."

"Believe me, I'd love nothing more, but you need your rest. You're still not fully recovered, and today was... Well, you know what today was. Plus...my dad is here."

"You're a grown woman, Aspen."

"I know that. So does he. Still... It's a little weird, don't you think?"

"The only thing that would be weird to me is not sleeping next to the woman I love." He stalks toward me, takes me in his arms, and gives me a passionate kiss.

I open for him.

I can't not.

He's so much a part of me, and he gives me so much comfort.

My door, of course, is still cracked open.

And my father... My father is somewhere in this house. I don't know if he's gone to bed yet.

But if he has? He's somewhere in this hallway.

I break the kiss. "Buck..."

"Please, baby. I need you. After the day we've both had, we need each other."

He's not wrong.

"All right," I sigh. "Close my door. And lock it."

"Absolutely." He inches back toward the door, closes and locks it, and then he comes back to me, cups my cheek. "You're so beautiful, Aspen. I'm so sorry about today. About what you had to go through."

"It's okay. I feel like a weight has been lifted off my shoulders. I know who set me up now, and they're going to pay."

"They will. I promise you that they will."

"I suppose Greg Wallace is already paying. I wish I knew which one he was."

"Do you really need to know that?"

"I suppose not. Gloria... She was innocent, and now she's dead."

"She was innocent with regard to setting you up. But she *did* lie to us. She knew those two voices she heard talking were Taylor and Nancy. If she had leveled with us, we could've protected her. Kept her safe. And she and her husband would still be alive."

"She was afraid."

"Of course she was afraid. But whatever kind of connections this Greg Wallace has from prison, they're nothing compared to the kind of connections the Wolfes or Luke have."

"I suppose they're not."

"So if she had leveled with us, we would've known she might be in danger, and we could've protected her and Brian both."

I nod. He's right, of course. And frankly, Gloria wasn't the person I always thought she was. She did have negative feelings toward me, even if she hated herself for it.

But would *I* have felt any differently? If I'd been all but promised middle blocker, and then some newbie swooped in and took it right from under me?

I'm not the devout Catholic girl Gloria was. I would've had some *very* negative feelings. But the world of pro sports is brutal. We all knew that. I would've come to terms with it. And I certainly wouldn't have sold my opponent off to some island to live as a slave.

That wasn't Gloria, of course. I don't think she ever would've done that. That was Taylor and Nancy...and Greg Wallace.

Damn...

Greg Wallace.

I turn to Buck. "I want to see Greg Wallace."

He furrows his brow. "Baby... Come on."

"I have to. I need to ask him questions. I need to find out—"

He pushes two fingers over my mouth to quiet me. "Isn't this enough, baby? Please? We know who was behind it, and they're all going to pay. Wallace is already paying, Taylor paid with her life, and Nancy's going to pay. Katelyn's tormentor, Chris Pollack, is finally going to pay because he killed Gloria and Brian."

Still, my nerves jump under my skin. There's something more I need to know.

And Greg Wallace can tell me.

"Please, Buck. I need to talk to him. You can arrange it. Or Luke can."

"Anyone can visit a prisoner. Of course it can be arranged. But Aspen, it's not a good idea."

"Please."

"What would your father say?"

"We can ask him."

"That's not the point I was trying to make. Your father wants you safe. He wants you healing. You can heal now. You've got your revenge. All the people behind your abduction are either dead or are going to spend the rest of their lives in prison."

"No," I say, beginning to pace around the room. "It's not enough, Buck. I need to know everything."

29

BUCK

Yep.

I never doubt my hunches.

I had a feeling this wasn't over.

And I was right.

Aspen is not going to let this lie. At least not yet.

Frankly, I'm glad Darnell is here. He and I will chat in the morning. Hopefully he'll be able to talk Aspen out of continuing this.

Why would she want to see Greg Wallace? He's a psychopath. A psychopath spending his life behind bars.

Apparently he couldn't buy his way out like some of the other billionaires from that island.

If only I could fuck this need out of her.

But this is Aspen Davis. I can fuck her until the sun comes up, and I plan to, but none of that will change her mind.

"I'm serious," Aspen says again. "I need to know everything."

I grab her then. Meet her gaze and stare into those fiery brown eyes.

"You're going to try to talk me out of it, aren't you?"

"Hell no," I say. "I'm not going to talk at all."

I crush my mouth to hers.

She opens for me, which is not totally unexpected.

The chemistry between us has always sizzled, and we can't resist each other.

She's wrapped in a robe, and already my cock is hard for her.

I rake my fingers through her short hair, massage her scalp, and then I let one hand drop to the robe's sash and untie it.

Then with both hands, I brush it off her shoulders. It falls into a puddle on the floor.

She's naked then. Naked in my arms, and without breaking our kiss, I lead her to the bed.

The door is locked. I don't know where Darnell is, and he's certainly not at the front of my mind right now.

Nope. Lover's six-foot six father? Big boner killer.

I wipe that from my mind.

This will be hard and fast. We're good at that.

But first—

I spread her legs, and I touch between them.

She's wet for me.

I inhale. She smells fresh, like soap and woman.

But between her legs is the ultimate delicacy. Her. Aspen. My beautiful Aspen.

I suck on her clit, thrust two fingers inside her, and she shoots, climaxing around my fingers.

That didn't take long.

Not that I expected it to, after the day we had. She's clamoring for release, and so am I.

I pull my cock out of my lounge pants, climb atop her,

thrust inside.

Sweet, sweet relief.

I won't be able to last either.

I pull out and thrust back in. Again. Again. Again.

Until—

"God!"

I release. I come. I give her everything. Everything in me. Everything—my heart, my soul—shoots out through my cock and into her.

The end of her climax and the beginning of mine, and as we soar together, reality hits me in the head.

I love this woman, but she won't stop.

She won't stop until she's done.

So I have a choice.

Do I help her? Or do I hinder her?

Already I know the answer.

She's my forever. I love her. And until she's happy? I won't be happy.

When the contractions finally cease and relaxation sweeps over me, I roll off of her. I turn on my side, my head on my shoulder.

"Baby?"

She opens her eyes and turns her head to look at me. "That was amazing," she says.

"It was."

Then she closes her eyes again.

"Baby?"

She opens them. "Yeah?"

"Whatever you need. I'm here for you. If you want to talk to Greg Wallace, I'll make it happen."

"Really?"

"I'm not saying I think it's a good idea, baby. But I understand you. I understand you need more answers."

"I do. And thank you."

It's not a lie. I *do* understand her need. I just think that sometimes there are more important things than the need for answers.

Like getting on with your life. Healing. Moving forward, not backward.

It took me a long time to understand that. Because I used to be exactly like Aspen.

Honor, courage, and commitment.

It's what we learn as SEALs.

It's why I did not break—why I did not give away my secrets—even during the most brutal punishment I've ever received.

And it's what keeps me together now.

Humiliation threatens to overtake me.

But I control it.

I stay outside of myself. I do not focus inward.

I focus only on what I learned in training—how to control my emotions and my actions, regardless of circumstance.

The humiliation does not define me.

What someone else did to me does not define me.

My pain does not define me.

And I will not succumb.

Moments pass, and I drift in and out of consciousness.

I've lost a lot of blood. Will I even make it through this?

I open my eyes.

A light. Bright light, and a tunnel.

Peace is in that light. Peace and tranquility and no more pain. No more humiliation.

Tempting. So tempting—

"Buck!" A harsh whisper.

The light disappears.

Phoenix. His face. It's blurry, but it's him.

"Come on. Let's get out of here."

"How?"

"Friends on the inside. The insurgents have been...detained. We don't have much time."

I'm naked, and I make it to my feet.

Only then, through my blurred vision, do I realize that Leif is naked too.

"Clothes?

"Waiting for us. Guards' clothes."

"Guards' clothes?"

I can pass as an Afghan with my dark hair and dark eyes, tanned skin. But Leif? Phoenix? He's a blond and blue-eyed Scandinavian.

I don't ask the question. He'll find a way. The phoenix always rises.

The door to my cell is open, and Phoenix pulls me through it.

"Are you okay?" he asks.

Am I okay? What a loaded question. Surely they did as much to Ramsey as they did to me. And I can be as strong as the next person.

"Fine," I groan, ignoring the pain shooting through my legs, my shoulders, my ass. "Let's just get the fuck out of here."

Several guards lie unconscious in a heap in the hallway.

The other prisoners taunt us, but we pay them no mind.

They yell at us in foreign languages, sometimes in English. "Take us with you! Please!"

It hurts me to ignore their pleas, but I have no choice.

I'm on a mission, and the mission comes first.

"Come on. That one looks about your size." Phoenix gestures to one of the unconscious guards.

"Right." I get to work, undressing the guard and praying he won't wake.

I put on his clothing and take everything, including his firearms.

Phoenix does the same.

"Your eyes," I whisper.

"Already taken care of." He dons a pair of shades. I have no idea where he got them, and I don't ask.

More pain lances through me.

But I won't let any of it stop me.

They will not take me alive.

And they will not get any information out of me.

I held up during the worst torture imaginable.

But I'm not naïve. I know how much more they could do.

We stalk quietly through the pathways toward an open door, brandishing the guards' weapons.

"We may have to separate," Phoenix says.

I nod.

"Once we're out, get to safety. Anywhere. We'll find each other."

"The others?" I ask.

"Wolf's already out."

Wolf. Bobby Ensign. Big and strong Bobby.

Footsteps advance toward us.

"See you on the outside," Phoenix turns right, while I go left.

I run straight into—

A freaking insurgent.

I don't think.

I don't have time to think.

I shoot him dead with his pal's gun and hurry on my way.

30

ASPEN

The next morning, we dress for the arraignment.

Both Nancy and Pollack will be arraigned today. I'm not even sure what they're charging Nancy with.

I wish they'd throw the damned book at her, even though technically she didn't kill anyone. But she was party to my abduction.

Luke made sure we all had decent clothes to wear.

Buck is dressed in a suit. A dark gray suit, white button-down shirt, blue tie. Polished leather shoes. And my God, he looks like he could be walking a runway.

Does he even have a clue how good-looking he is? What the hell does he see in me?

I'm wearing a navy-blue skirt and a cream-colored blouse. Simple black pumps. Not really my style, but we have to look the part to go to court.

My father's dressed in a navy-blue suit with a red tie. Katelyn is dressed similarly to me, except that her skirt is a lighter blue and her blouse pink. Luke is in a dark suit. Nearly black. White shirt, green tie.

All looking the part.

We arrive at the courthouse in Luke's black SUV—the same SUV he took when he went to Gloria's house.

We use the valet parking, and then we make our way into the courthouse, through electronic screening. Katelyn and I push our purses through the scanner.

We're not armed. We can't be armed and come in the courthouse. But security is rampant here—if they can be trusted.

I don't trust anyone. There's always someone who can be bought.

Courtroom J.

Another arraignment is taking place, but Pollack and Nancy are next on the docket.

Just as we walk in, the judge pounds her gavel. "Five minute recess." She rises and leaves her podium.

We find seats close to the prosecution side.

The prosecutor shakes our hands. "Thank you for being here."

"Just put this man away," Luke says.

"I'll do my best."

A few minutes later, the bailiff says, "All rise."

We stand.

"Superior Court of Los Angeles is now in session, the Honorable Priscilla Barnes presiding."

The judge takes her seat. "You may be seated."

"We have the arraignment of Christopher James Pollack," she says, "also known as Louis Stanley McCain."

So that's his real name. Whatever.

The bailiff brings Pollack in. He's clad in an orange jumpsuit, and his hair is a scraggly mess. His yellow eyes are swollen and bloodshot.

"Jonathan Myers for the prosecution," the prosecutor says.

"Bridget Bagley from the public defender's office for the defendant," opposing counsel says.

"All right." Judge Barnes scans her documents. "Mr. Pollack, you're accused of two counts of murder in the first degree. One count of assault and battery with intent to kill. How do you plead?"

Guilty.

Luke told us this morning that Pollack had agreed to plead guilty.

Pollack, his hands bound, clears his throat.

"I'm waiting," the judge says.

"Not guilty, your honor."

"Jesus Christ," Buck says under his breath.

"Wasn't he supposed to plead guilty?" I ask.

"That's what I thought." He glares at Luke.

"All right, not guilty it is," Judge Barnes make some notes. "Ms. Bagley?"

"We ask that the defendant be released on his own recognizance," Ms. Bagley says.

Judge Barnes laughs. She actually laughs. "Yeah, that's not going to happen."

"Your Honor," Myers says, "we ask that the defendant be held without bail. He's currently under immunity from the federal courts, but with this new crime, that has been revoked. He will go to prison one way or the other. Due to the extraneous issues in this case, we also request a speedy trial."

"I can't think of a better place for him," Judge Barnes says. "Ms. Bagley, your request is denied. Mr. Pollack will be held without bail pending any additional hearings. I will be granting the prosecution's request for a speedy trial. Trial date is set for next month."

"Next month?" I whisper to Buck.

"That's actually damned speedy," he says. "I guess we're staying in LA for a while."

"Why didn't he—"

The bailiff interrupts me. "Next on the docket: State of California versus Margo Caprice, also known as Nancy Louise Mosely."

Nancy comes in then, also in an orange jumpsuit and also bound at the wrists. Her dirty blond hair hangs in strings over her shoulders.

"Jonathan Myers for the prosecution, your honor."

"And Bridget Bagley for the defense."

"Ms. Caprice," Judge Barnes says, "you are accused of one count of kidnapping. How do you plead?"

"Ms. Mosely would like a plea agreement, your honor," Bagley says.

"All right. Has the prosecution agreed to one?"

"We have, your honor," Myers says. "We've agreed to six months jail time and three years' probation."

"Very well."

"Wait a minute!" I rise.

"Ma'am," Judge Barnes says, "I'm going to have to ask you to remain seated."

"You don't know what she did to me. The hell I've been through, and the—"

"I'm sorry, ma'am, but you're going to have to sit down. I cannot allow disruptions in my courtroom."

"But I was sent to that island! By her! And I—"

Buck rises, pulls me into his arm, kisses my forehead.

"Aspen, please. She can send you to jail. We'll get through this." He grabs my hand and leads me out of the courtroom. "I'm sorry, baby," he says. "You can't just talk to a judge like that."

"It's a woman judge. She'll understand."

"Maybe she will. But do you want to take that chance? I don't want you spending a night in jail."

He's right, of course. I know better. It's just... "Pollack was supposed to plead guilty."

"I know, but it's okay. No jury will dare not convict him after we all testify."

"I suppose not. And then he'll get what's coming to him."

"He will. You need to trust the system."

"All right."

But I *don't* trust the system.

Katelyn comes out a moment later, tears streaming down her face, Luke holding her hand.

"It's okay, sweetheart," Luke says. "I promise you this will be okay."

"But he was supposed to be sent away. Today."

"I know. I'll take care of this."

Buck looks at Luke.

Katelyn looks at me.

Something is brewing.

I don't know what it is, but perhaps Pollack will get what's coming to him without a trial.

31

BUCK

Darnell drives home to Colorado. There's no reason for him to stay here for a month while we wait for the trial date.

Katelyn and Aspen are both distraught, and they decide to have some wine on the deck and play with the dogs.

Just as well.

Luke and I need to talk.

Once we're in his office, I start the conversation. "What are you going to do about this?"

He raises his eyebrows. "You're not asking me to break the law, are you?"

"What if I am?"

"Then I'll tell you that my immunity deal is contingent upon me being a law-abiding citizen."

"Right. Even though you held Chris Pollack in a safe-house and—"

"However"—he gestures for me to stop as he clears his throat—"I do know people who *will* break the law. For a price."

"A price that can't be traced back to us?"

"Aren't you the honorable military man," he says with a wry smile.

"Shut the fuck up, Raven—"

His jaw clenches. "Wait just a fucking minute."

I hold up a hand. "That's who you are to me and who you always will be. But this matters to you just as much as it does to me. Pollack is the man who tortured your fiancée. And he's also the man who killed Gloria Delgado and her husband. He's not a good man."

"Do you hear me arguing?"

"What can we do about it?"

"I'm looking into it. But I can't make any promises. My new life—my life with Katelyn—means everything to me."

I say nothing. I understand. My life with Aspen means everything to me too. Of course *I'm* not under the pressure of an immunity deal.

Still, I *am* an honorable man. A Navy SEAL. I can't do what I want to do here.

Damn.

Damn, damn, damn.

"All right, on another subject then."

"What?" Luke asks.

"Aspen wants to talk to Greg Wallace."

Luke's eyebrows rise. "What the hell for?"

"She wants more information about how she ended up on that island."

"I think it's pretty clear by now. Nancy and Taylor orchestrated it. Taylor went to her uncle, her uncle was familiar with the island, and that gave them a chance to get rid of Aspen. Taylor's father found out and disowned her. She's lucky that's all he did."

"Right. But Aspen's not satisfied yet."

"You mean her need for revenge isn't satisfied."

"Honestly, I'm not sure if that's what it is anymore. I think she just wants answers. She deserves that much, Luke."

"It's Luke now?"

"Look. You and I are never going to like each other. That is just a fact."

"You're wrong about that, Moreno. I *do* like you. I like you because of what you did for Katelyn. She may not have survived that mess without you."

"I'm not so sure that's true. Katelyn has an inner strength that isn't always visible on the outside."

"Yeah," Luke says. "You're right about that. She's an amazing woman."

"So is Aspen. And I want her to have closure. Even though I don't fucking believe in closure."

"Are you sure she's up for it? To see this person?"

"No. But she's strong. She's as strong as anyone I've ever known."

"Wallace is a psychopath."

"A psychopath on steroids," I agree. "And I'll be with her. You can count on that."

"All right," Luke says. "I have connections. I can get the two of you a visit with Greg Wallace."

"How soon?"

"Probably within a day or two. But only if you're sure."

Hell no, I'm not sure. I think this may be a mistake. But I'd do just about anything for Aspen.

"I'm sure," I say.

~

"WE'RE GOING to have a fun day," Katelyn says the next day at breakfast.

Aspen and I meet each other's gaze. A fun day? With everything else that's going on?

"Yeah," Katelyn says. "I can tell by the looks on your faces that you're just as excited about it as I am."

Right.

"I'm serious. I already told Luke this morning. We're going to go to the beach."

"Katelyn," Aspen says, "the beach is in your backyard."

"Right. Except we're going to go to a public beach."

I cock my head. "Why would we go to a public beach when you've got a private beach right here?"

Katelyn huffs. "Because we need a day off from this, damn it. We need a day where we can just"—she sighs—"*be*."

I can't agree with her more, to be honest. For Aspen, that is. She needs to relax. I had hoped her need for answers would be sated when she found out the truth.

It's not.

Now she wants to talk to Greg Wallace, which Luke said he would set up. I almost hoped he'd say he couldn't do it. But he understands Aspen's need for knowledge.

I do too. I just love her so much and I want her out of danger. And that includes mental and emotional danger as well.

"We'll take the dogs," Katelyn says.

"The dogs?" I raise my eyebrows.

"Yes, of course. There are dog-friendly beaches here in LA. We're going to go to one. We're going to lie on beach towels instead of lounge chairs, and we're going to have a simple day of relaxation. Like normal people."

"All right." Aspen rises, takes the last drink of her coffee, and sets the mug down. “Katelyn, if this is important to you, let’s go to the freaking beach.”

“Good.” Katelyn nods. “I took the liberty of having several bathing suits sent over. You can choose the one you like best.” She turns to me. “You too, Buck.”

“As long as they’re not Speedos.”

Aspen gushes. “Seriously, Buck? You’d look amazing in a Speedo.”

“Yeah. Not happening. I’m also not shaving all the hair off my body and oiling up.”

“God, no,” Aspen says. “No shaving. I love your chest hair.”

“I didn’t order Speedos,” Katelyn says. “Luke hates them. I ordered several pairs of trunks, in your size. They’re in your room.”

Luke is nowhere around.

“Are you sure Luke’s okay with this?” I ask. “I notice he’s not here.”

“He had a few phone calls he had to make this morning, but he will be out in a moment. He promised to come along.”

Aspen’s features have softened a bit. Perhaps this is exactly what she needs. A day of leisure at the beach. At a regular old beach, the kind of beaches she and I are used to. A place where only a towel separates us from the sand of the earth.

This private beach thing? It’s great, but it’s not really us.

“All right, baby,” I say, “let’s get ready to go to the beach.”

32

ASPEN

I chose a tankini. I've never liked one-piece bathing suits. I hate that you have to take the whole thing off to go to the bathroom. But a bikini? I'm not quite ready to show the world my scars. I have enough of them on my legs. I don't really want to display my torso and back to the world.

The tankini is green, and it pushes my tits up so I look like I have more than I do.

Buck's eyes nearly popped out of his head when he saw me.

He looks amazing as well in navy-blue trunks. They cover up too much of his muscular thighs, but I can't see him in a Speedo either.

Correction. I'd like very much to see him in a Speedo, but it's really not him.

We're not technically at a public beach. It's a semiprivate beach. We had to pay to get in, and I'm just as glad. Public beaches tend to be crowded, even on weekdays like today. Plus, even though Luke brought a security team—of course—we're safer here than at an actual public beach.

Katelyn called ahead and rented a cabana, so we have a place to hang out if we want to get out of the sun. Plus, wait staff visit us from time to time so we can order drinks and snacks.

Katelyn is also wearing a tankini, most likely to cover her scars as well. She doesn't have as many as I do, at least not on her legs. I haven't seen the rest of her.

Luke wears a pair of red, white, and blue trunks, and he looks pretty good as well. He's not quite as muscular as Buck, but he's a fine specimen. His hair is starting to grow out. Apparently he likes to wear it long.

The most interesting thing about looking at Buck and Luke in trunks is their tattoos. Buck has the SEAL trident on his arm of course, and then the elaborate tattoo on his back in honor of his fallen friends.

Luke's tattoo is beautiful as well. It starts on his left hand, swirls up his arm and becomes a Raven with flaming wings that stretches out onto his shoulder and upper back.

It's the tattoo he kept secret from Katelyn when they first met.

Two amazing men here.

With completely opposite pasts, but who are the best of the best.

Truly good men.

If I were a better person, I'd let this all go. I'd leave these two men to be good men. I wouldn't insist on seeing Greg Wallace.

But I can't help it.

It all seems so unfinished to me.

Maybe it's just because Pollack didn't enter the guilty plea that he had agreed to, and now we have to stay around here for a trial. I'll have to get up on the stand and tell my harrowing story in front of a jury.

And I'm wondering...

Maybe that's what he wants.

Maybe he's punishing me.

Sure, he has to spend the rest of his life in prison. He screwed up his immunity deal. I get that he was forced to do it, but so what? It's his own fault he was obsessed with Katelyn and went after Luke.

Besides, no one forced him to go on that island and do what he did to Katelyn.

Does he really think he has a shot at getting off at a trial?

And then I look around.

We're not on a public beach...but it's only semiprivate.

If the witnesses go away—Luke, Katelyn, Buck, and I—plus Nancy—they'll have to drop the charges against Pollack.

Damn.

That's it.

That's why he didn't plead guilty.

He's going to try to have us eliminated.

And I realize...

Buck and Luke have probably already thought of this. Whether they've put it into words? Or even a passing thought? I don't know. But they know. They know what Pollack must be thinking. Hence the security contingent watching discreetly over us.

I'm alone in the cabana right now, but Buck is approaching me, coming back from a swim. His hair is plastered to his cheeks and neck, and water drips over him, pasting his trunks against his muscular thighs.

He looks completely luscious.

He reaches for a towel.

"Buck..."

"Yeah, baby?"

"I just had a thought."

"What kind of thought?

"Of why Pollack might have refused to plead guilty."

"I'm sure it's a thought I've already had."

"He's going to try to have us eliminated, isn't he?"

Buck rubs the towel over his head. "He can try."

"He's in prison now, awaiting trial. He's going to have all kinds of connections."

"No," Buck says. "Luke and I have talked about this. The connections in prison won't be any good to him. Pollack's a canary. They don't like canaries in prison. They also don't like people who abuse and torture women. Rapists aren't treated well in prison."

"I suppose not. But still—"

"Don't worry about it, baby. They're keeping him in the county jail while he awaits trial. Luke and I just found that out this morning. They're concerned about the risk to him if they take him to the prison."

I drop my jaw. "So there won't be any connections. That's what he was hoping for."

"Yup. But even he knew—or if he didn't, he's just stupid—that there was probably a mark on his head if they sent him to the prison."

"So you think we're okay?"

"Luke has twenty-four-seven security—the best money can buy. And *I'm* your security, Aspen."

"Paid for by the Wolfes."

He smiles. "Do you really think they have to pay me at this point? I will always be your security, Aspen. As long as I'm with you, I will not allow anything to happen to you."

I throw my arms around him, kiss him on his lips. "Thank you so much."

"You don't need to thank me for protecting the woman I love. It's a pleasure. Besides, I can't live without you now."

"I can't live without you either. Sometimes I wonder how I got so lucky. How can someone as good as you, as honorable as you, love me?"

"How can I not? You're as good and honorable as I am."

He's sweet to say it, but it's not true. If I were truly good and honorable, I would be done now. I found out the story behind my kidnapping, and the people behind it are either dead or will be brought to justice. So why am I still searching for answers?

Before I can think too much about it, though, one of the waitstaff assigned to our cabana, a young woman named Kathy, approaches us.

"Would you two care to order any lunch?"

Katelyn and Luke arrive, dripping from the water.

"Lunchtime," Luke says.

"I was just about to take an order from these two," Kathy says.

"Could I see a menu?" Katelyn asks.

"Certainly." Kathy hands her a laminated menu.

"Do you have just a regular burger?" I ask. "Cheddar cheese, lettuce, tomato, onion. Side of fries?"

"You got it. And a drink?"

"I'm thinking a nice freshly-brewed iced tea," I say.

"I'll have the same," Buck says. "Except bring me a nice freshly-brewed beer on tap."

Kathy laughs. "Absolutely."

"Ditto for me," Luke says. "Except not the beer. I'll take the iced tea."

"I like to be different," Katelyn says. "I'd like the chicken sandwich please, grilled not fried, and a side salad. Iced tea as well."

"Got it all," Kathy says. "I'll bring these out as soon as they're ready."

Buck turns to me. "A burger, huh?"

"Yeah, I'm feeling pretty hungry, actually. Haven't had a burger in...I don't know how long."

"I was surprised you didn't order the fish tacos," Katelyn chuckles.

"No, I still can't get the taste for seafood. I know I ordered them at our lunch, but I had to force them down. I just felt that if I could eat fish tacos, I could accomplish anything. Silly, I know."

"Are you kidding me?" Katelyn says. "It wasn't silly. It was strong. You got them down. You did it."

"I did. And I didn't throw up afterward. But it'll be a long time before I order them again. I can't even think about it."

"Or 'taco' about it?" Buck raises his eyebrows.

I look around for something to throw at him. "Taco. Talk. Was that supposed to be a joke?"

"A poor attempt, obviously," he says, smiling.

We all laugh then.

And it's kind of strange, really, for all of us to be laughing.

Since the four of us have been together, maybe one or two of us has forced out a chuckle at one time or another, but for all four of us to laugh at the same time? I think this is the first time it's happened.

It feels pretty good.

After lunch, I grab Edgar. "We're going to take a walk on the beach."

"Want some company?" Buck asks.

"Absolutely."

We leave Katelyn, Luke, and Jed, and amble to the water's edge.

Hand-in-hand, Buck and I walk, while I hold Edgar's leash with my other hand. He puts his paws in the water, but that's as far as he goes.

He's a good boy. Gloria and Brian obviously trained him well. He comes when he is called, and he knows all the other commands—sit, stay, speak.

At the beach house, he never leaves the radius of about twenty feet from Buck and me. I'm not even sure he needs a leash.

At least there's something I can do for Gloria. I can take care of her dog, love her dog.

I believe Gloria was a good person. So she had jealous feelings for me. Envious feelings. That doesn't make her a bad person. It makes her human. She didn't deserve to die for that.

Gloria didn't ask Taylor and Nancy to do what they did. She did try to protect them though. I mean, at the time, she was in a relationship with Taylor. And Nancy? I don't really know what Gloria's feelings for Nancy were.

There is still so much I don't understand.

Why did Greg Wallace force Nancy to marry Taylor? Nancy claims she's not gay, and now that I think about it… I wasn't on the team for very long, but I never saw her with another woman.

Of course I didn't see her with a man either.

Brandon came to one of our games, and some of the other players' significant others would show up now and then. But no one ever showed up for Nancy, at least not that I can remember. Of course I wasn't on the team for long.

That doesn't mean anything. If she says she's not gay, I'll take her statement at face value. It was clear that she and Taylor weren't in love, anyway.

Greg Wallace will have those answers.

Will he be forthright with me?

I have no idea. The man is a psychopath. A criminal. Serving a life sentence for what he did on that island. Serving a life sentence because Chris Pollack snitched on him.

No wonder they're keeping Pollack at the county jail. If they ship him off to prison, he'll be dead in twenty-four hours.

"What are you thinking about?" Buck asks. "You're being quiet."

The warm ocean breeze drifts over us, and Buck's hair flows gently. It's dry now, and he has that polished-by-salt-water look about him.

Part of me wishes the beach were empty, so we could lie down in the soft sand and make love.

Of course, that's just a fantasy. Making love in the sand is anything but sexy. The tiny grains get everywhere. Brandon and I tried it once when we were vacationing in Florida.

I sigh. "I'm wondering… Once you find answers, there are always more questions."

"I know, baby."

"Why didn't you warn me?"

"What would've been the point?"

I can't help but laugh. He's right of course. I had it in my mind that I was going to find these people and make them pay. I've done that, but I still have so many questions.

"Thank you for standing by me," I say. "For putting up with my quest."

"My place is at your side, Aspen. It has been since I first laid eyes on you."

I smile as warmth gushes through me. "I didn't take you for a romantic, Buck. Do you really believe in love at first sight?"

"Love took a few days," he says. "But I certainly believe in being knocked off my feet at first sight, and you sure as hell did that to me."

"You did that to me too, and I never thought I'd ever let a man touch me again."

"I wasn't sure I *should* touch you, baby. But you… How could I resist you? You're everything. You're so beautiful."

"I never thought I was beautiful."

"Are you kidding me? That face, that body. Everything about you. Your beautiful brown eyes are so big and round. You look like a Disney princess."

I raise my eyebrows and stop in my tracks. "A Disney princess?"

"Your eyes are so big and brown. Your lashes are so long."

"Wait a minute. You watch Disney princesses?"

"You going to give me a hard time about that?"

I laugh. "I absolutely am."

"Of course you are." He squeezes my hand. "I wouldn't have you any other way. And for the record, I don't watch a lot of Disney, but the princesses are everywhere, baby. I grew up with a little sister who loved Cinderella and Belle and all of them. Plus, we've been in LA for only a little over a week, and how many billboards have we seen with Disney princesses on them? Every time I see one of them with their big doe eyes, I think of you. You could've been the model for Belle in *Beauty and the Beast.*"

"Now I *know* you're kidding me."

"Why do you doubt me? Do you really think I'd be talking to you about Disney princesses if I weren't telling you the truth?"

He has a point there.

"I've never seen a Disney princess with short hair," I say.

"Rapunzel has short hair at the end of *Tangled*."

I laugh. I laugh hard, and man, it feels good. "You know entirely *too* much about Disney princesses."

"I know that you'd make a perfect one. Seriously, you could be Belle."

"My skin's a little darker than Belle's."

"Okay, Jasmine then."

"My skin's a little lighter than Jasmine's."

"You're bound and determined to fight me on this, aren't you?"

"I suppose I am. You see, Buck, things that have happened to me just don't happen to Disney princesses."

"That's not exactly true," Buck says. "You've had it much worse of course, but Belle was kidnapped by a beast. Rapunzel was locked in a tower. Sleeping Beauty was put into a coma. So was Snow White."

"You do watch the movies." I give him a good-natured punch on the arm.

"I watched most of them when I was a kid."

I shake my head, smiling. "I suppose the Disney princesses didn't have it much easier than I have. Of course, the fact remains that they're not real."

"I know, baby. I'm just trying to lighten up the situation. No Disney princesses were subjected to the horrors you've been subjected to. But none of that negates your beauty, Aspen. You're even more beautiful than any Disney princess. You're the most beautiful woman I've ever laid eyes on."

Disney princesses are drawings, but I can't help but take Buck's words as a compliment.

Even though I've never been beautiful, not in that sense.

But perhaps beauty truly is in the eye of the beholder.

No one can say that Buck isn't beautiful. He is. And yes, men can be beautiful. I could call him handsome, but that's not quite right. Magnificent, which he is, but it still doesn't do him justice.

Gorgeous? We're getting closer. Majestic? Closer still.

But he truly is beautiful. Perfect masculine beauty.

I squeeze his hand. "Thank you."

"For what?"

"For loving me. For thinking I'm beautiful. For thinking I look like a Disney princess."

"You don't have to thank me for any of that. I can't help loving you, baby. I didn't even know I was searching for you until I found you."

I smile, except it's more than a smile on my lips. It's a smile that goes deep inside me, to my heart and my soul. "It's the same way for me. I didn't think I would ever love again, didn't think I'd ever want to be touched again. But you..."

He stops, pulls me toward him, as Edgar flurries around our feet. In a moment, we're kissing, a deep tongue kiss, and for that one moment, everyone else on the beach?

Even Edgar?

They all disappear.

Buck and I are alone, in a bubble.

A perfect and wonderful and safe bubble.

I melt into his kiss, let it take me somewhere else.

Somewhere where there are no more questions. Only answers.

Only Buck. And only me.

And of course Edgar.
His fur tickles my ankles.
I began laughing, and the kiss breaks.
And I think...
This may just be a perfect day.

33

BUCK

"I got you in," Luke says the next morning. "You and Aspen can go see Greg Wallace this afternoon at three p.m."

I'm seated across from Luke in his office. "That was quick."

It's not quite noon. Aspen and I have only been up for a few hours.

After a day at the beach, we were both so relaxed that we made love all night and then slept in.

Luke clears his throat. "Actually it wasn't difficult. The assistant warden at the California State Prison is an old friend of my father's."

"So you didn't have to call in any of your connections?"

"Well, he *is* a connection. Just one that's aboveboard. Katelyn will be happy about that."

I draw in a breath. "*I'm* happy about that. I would really love for all of this to be aboveboard from here on out."

"Believe it or not," Luke says, "so would I. I'm determined

to live an honorable life, Buck, whether you believe me or not."

I *do* believe him. I just don't want to give him the satisfaction of telling him that I do.

"For what it's worth," I say, "thank you. I really don't want to do this, but it's important to Aspen."

"She'll come around," he says. "You can only get so many answers before you decide it's not worth it anymore."

"Spoken like a man who knows what he's talking about."

"You have no idea," he says.

"Actually, I think I do."

"It may surprise you to know that we're not all that different," Luke continues. "You may have lived an honorable life in the military, and I lived a dishonorable life underground in the drug trade, but our lives probably weren't all that different."

I cross my arms over my chest. "Not sure I can agree with you there."

"I don't expect you to agree. Let's just say I know what it's like to have to leave a fallen man behind."

I don't ask him to elaborate, and I know he doesn't expect me to.

"Do you want to come along? To see Wallace?" I ask when I stand.

"No." He shakes his head. "I'm done with this. For Katelyn's sake. It will always live on inside her, and consequently, it will also live inside me. But we're moving on. We're going to set a wedding date soon."

"Oh?"

"Yes, and it goes without saying that we would like to have you and Aspen there."

"I know Aspen wouldn't miss it. And neither will I."

I may have no love for Luke, but I do love Katelyn. And if this makes her happy? I will be there to celebrate with her. With Aspen at my side, and perhaps with a ring on her finger by then.

AFTER SURRENDERING everything in our possession but our firstborn child, Aspen and I are led by a guard into the visitation room.

I'm surprised, actually. I expected to see Wallace behind one of those Plexiglas bulletproof windows talking through a phone receiver.

In the room, we're led to a table with three chairs.

"Do I have your guarantee that we'll be safe out here?" I ask the guard who escorts us.

"Absolutely. Do you think we'd let these derelicts out here if we couldn't guarantee your safety?"

"Man, I just don't know." I case the room quickly.

Guards are stationed throughout the perimeter, and some inmates are already in the room, talking to their visitors at tables like the one we're sitting at.

"We'll be fine, Buck." Aspen takes a seat.

Strength emanates from her. I know she's scared, and I know she's worried, but you could never tell it by looking at her.

She's so amazing.

"The inmate will be out in a few moments. His hands and his feet will be bound. And even though no weapons are allowed in prison, he will have been thoroughly searched—and I mean thoroughly—before he's allowed in this room."

"Good." I take the seat next to Aspen. "Thank you very much for all your help."

"Absolutely. I'll go retrieve the inmate."

The guard—his name tag says Buckley—leaves then, exiting through a door after he slides a card through a lock.

Aspen bites on her lower lip.

"You okay?"

She nods. "I am. I just have so many questions."

"I understand. But I don't want you to be upset if you don't get any answers from this guy. Or if the answers you get are lies."

"I know. I've thought of all of that."

"Okay."

The door opens. I look up, but Aspen looks down at the table.

Buckley returns with an oddly pale man. "Here you are. These are the people who want to talk to you, Albino."

"Albino?" I say.

"Sorry. Wallace. This is Greg Wallace."

Aspen looks up.

And then she gasps.

"*You?*"

34

ASPEN

He smiles.

The man smiles.

One of his front teeth is missing.

It wasn't missing that day on the island. That day when he bit my nipple off my breast.

The pain comes searing back into my reality.

I close my eyes, swallow. Try to remain strong.

But time moves backward, backward, backward...

And I'm there, on the island, with him ordering me to get up and run. I remember.

I remember it all.

~

"Fucking bitch," he says, his pasty body covering mine. "You will get up, and you will run." He pulls me up, forces me into a standing position.

I let my legs buckle beneath me. "No. I'm done running from you."

He pulls me up again, gives me a push. Instinctually, I land on my feet. But then I drop to the ground.

He pulls me up again. I lose count of how many times he persists, while he slaps and punches me in between.

But I feel no pain.

I have decided. I will not give this man what he wants.

If I die here? So be it.

I know I won't die. Not if this man wants to come back to the island.

"Fine, bitch. We'll do it your way. But you'll be fucking sorry." He pulls on my left foot, twists my ankle.

I cry out in pain.

"You might want to save your voice, bitch. I'm just getting started." He curls both of his hands into fists then and punches my stomach—

I groan, trying to catch my breath.

But the wind has been punched out of me.

I've been punched before though, many times. Not just on the island, but on the volleyball court, by a rogue ball.

I can take this.

I can take it all.

He punches my jaw next, and the pain radiates through my skull.

Then my cheek, and my eye.

I'll have a black eye, but it won't be the first time. I've had a black eye from a volleyball too. And also on this island many times.

He's far from done, though. He's angry. Angry that I'm not letting him chase me.

Angry that I'm not playing the game by his rules.

A feeling of peace settles over me.

Oh, I'm still in pain. Probably more pain than I've ever been in my life, but I'm exerting my will. For the first time since I came onto this island, I'm exerting my will.

And though I may end up black and blue because of it, at least I'm not giving this asshole what he wants.

I take punch after punch to every part of my body.

Punch after punch after punch, and yes, I yell. Yes, I scream. Yes, I groan, but the peace never wavers. The peace. The knowledge that he's not getting his way.

Until—

Crack!

A searing pain so terrible and forceful that I cry out, my eyes closed.

Death is surely coming for me now.

It's my left leg, the lower part. He hit me with something hard —a rock, a log...I don't know, but there's no way he could have done this bare handed.

The bones. My bones.

The cracking of my bones.

That's the sound I just heard.

And I don't think I'll live through this.

"Take that, fucking cunt. Now you'll never run again."

My eyes are still closed, but then another searing pain.

And then liquid trickling over my right breast.

Blood. Must be blood.

I don't know what he's done, but my God, the pain.

"Serves you right, you little whore. Now you're deformed. Disfigured. No one will want you now."

Blackness descends.

Blessed blackness. Darkness.

Blessed...

~

ASPEN?

Aspen, baby? Are you all right?

Buck's voice.

I hear it, though I'm not sure where it's coming from.

It seems to be coming from above me.

But he's next to me, and across from me is—

I open my eyes.

Track lighting. Harsh track lighting.

And my head.

My head hurts.

Aspen? Baby?

Where am I?

Cool tile floor against my legs.

"Aspen."

Buck's face. It comes into view, blurry at first but then as beautiful as an angel.

Am I in heaven?

Of course not. Heaven wouldn't have a cold tile floor.

"Can you hear me?"

"Yes," I croak out.

"Thank God."

"What happened?"

"You fell off your chair," Buck says. "You hit your head pretty hard. Are you all right?"

"Yeah. I think so."

"Can you sit up?" He pulls me into his arms.

This is where I'm safe. In Buck's arms.

"What happened? You recognized him?"

I nod against his shoulder.

The pasty guy. He was so pale, now I understand why. The guard called him Albino. Is he a true albino? I have no idea. But who the hell cares?

"Where did he go?" I ask.

"They took him back."

I jerk out of Buck's arms. "No! I need to talk to him. I have questions."

"Baby, you lost consciousness. You fainted when you saw him."

"It's because... Buck, he's the one. He's the one who hurt me so badly. The one who bit my... It's gone because of him. My nipple, Buck. He took it."

Buck goes rigid. "That's the motherfucker who did that to you?"

I nod, gulping.

"Jesus Christ. I'll kill him."

I dart my gaze around the room. "You can't say that here. This place is full of guards."

"Guards who probably wouldn't mind seeing the motherfucker dead."

"Not by your hand, Buck. Not ever. You're not that guy."

His killing days are over, and I don't want him to go back down that path because of me.

"Get the guard. Bring him back. I'll be all right this time now that I know who to expect. Please."

"All right," Buck says. "I'll see what I can do."

35

BUCK

"Will you be okay here for moment?" I ask Aspen.

"Yeah. I'm okay. I just wasn't expecting it to be...*him*."

I kiss the top of her head. "All right. I'll be right back."

I approach one of the guards standing around the perimeter of the room. "Hey, I'm really sorry about what happened back there. It was someone she recognized, and she wasn't expecting to recognize him."

"Sorry about that," the guard says. "Is she okay?"

"Yeah, she's fine now."

"You need any medical assistance?"

"No, I don't think so."

Though we'll be stopping at urgent care on the way home for sure.

"But," I continue, "she would like to see Greg Wallace. Could you bring him back in?"

"The albino?"

"Yeah, I guess so. That's apparently what you guys call him."

"For sure. The dude can't be in the sun without a coating of sunscreen. And of course a guard has to be present whenever he slathers it all over his body. That's always fun."

"So he's a true albino?"

"Far as I can tell, yeah."

"Can you bring him back?" I ask.

"Let me check for you," the guard says. "The dude's a psycho, though, and that's saying a lot because most of the guys in here are psychos. But he's in a class all by himself."

"Believe me, I know."

Any man who would bite off a woman's nipple is definitely unhinged.

The guard walks over to another guard, presumably whoever's in charge. They converse under their breath.

He returns. "We're going to bring him back out. Besides, the albino hasn't ever had any visitors. If we don't let him come out again, he may never get out of that cell."

"I don't really have a problem with that," I say.

"Neither do I," the guard says. "But we get accused of humanitarian violations if we don't let our guys out to see visitors, and since this is the first and only one he's ever had..."

I scoff. "Right. Humanitarian violations."

"I'm on your page, man," he says. "These sociopaths violated so many human rights before they got in here. Frankly, I don't feel like they are entitled to any in return, but the law sees things differently." He turns. "I'll be right back."

I return to the table. Aspen is rubbing her temples.

"You okay?"

"Yeah. I really am. I need to do this, Buck. I'm sorry that I lost it."

"No reason to be sorry. You didn't expect to recognize him."

"It's just so... This is the guy who's responsible for me being taken. This is the guy who Taylor and Nancy went to. The guy who put me on that island. And then to find out... that he's the one..." She shakes her head. "I should have done an online search for his mugshot. Why didn't I think of that?"

"Because you're thinking about other things," I say. "I should have thought of it too, baby, but we've both been inundated with other stuff. "Do you think he knew who you were?"

"I don't know. I'm going to find out."

A few moments later, the original guard, Buckley, returns with Wallace.

Wallace is smiling a snakelike grin, and that missing front tooth... I'd like to take the man who took it from him out to dinner. Better yet, I'd like to personally remove every other tooth in his skull.

But I calm my rage.

Aspen needs me to be calm, and I will be here for her.

"You have fifteen minutes," Buckley says. He pushes Wallace down into a chair.

"To what do I owe the pleasure?" Wallace says. His voice is oddly high.

"Is that really his voice?" I ask Aspen.

"I don't remember it being quite so high," she says. "I wouldn't have found him quite so menacing with that voice."

Wallace's smile fades.

"You must've been purposefully lowering your voice on the island," Aspen says.

"What if I was?" This time his voice is an octave lower.

"Yes," Aspen says. "That I remember."

"Did you come here to gloat, bitch?"

Rage pulses out of me, from the marrow of my bones outward through all my pores. "Call her that again, and you won't have any more teeth left."

"Like you could do anything to me in here," he says.

"Do you think any of those guards will stop me? They hate you as much as I do."

He doesn't reply.

Sure, the guards have to obey the law, but I have a feeling that behind closed doors, the rules get pushed onto the back burner.

"Ask him what you want to ask him, baby," I say.

"*Baby?*" Wallace sticks with the low voice. "So she's yours now, huh?"

"She was never *yours*," I say. "So get that out of your head right now."

"I remember a certain time when she was mine," he says. "I remember enjoying myself immensely."

"Enjoying yourself by beating up on a woman?" I clench my jaw. "Raping a woman? You really are piece of shit."

"Yeah? Well I got a piece of her you'll never have." His gaze drops to Aspen's breasts.

I stand then, my hands curled into fists. I pull him up by the collar of his jumpsuit.

A guard walks briskly over. "Everything okay here?"

"He threatened to pull my teeth out," Wallace says.

"Yeah? Should I call a dentist?" The guard laughs.

"Aren't you supposed to protect me from this asshole?"

"Sure I am. Out here in the open, anyway." He turns to me. "Sir, I have to ask you to let this piece of shit go."

I release Wallace and push him back down in his chair. "Sorry," I murmur.

"Hey, I didn't ask you to be sorry. I just said you had to let him go."

I sit back down.

"Do I need to stay here for this visit?" the guard asks.

I shake my head. "I'm good."

He nods and walks back to his place near the wall.

I just wasted five minutes, and Aspen needs this time. She needs this time to ask questions, get answers. Though I doubt this man will be forthcoming.

"Go ahead," I say to her. "Ask what you need to ask. Our time is running out."

36

ASPEN

My skin is crawling. I can actually feel tiny invisible creatures pecking at my flesh.

I remember those light blue eyes. That pasty white skin. I never saw his hair, but it's the lightest blondish gray.

Completely colorless.

He really is an albino. That would explain his pasty skin.

"I don't have all day, darlin'." Wallace says.

"I'm hardly your darlin'," I say. "But I do need some answers to some questions. Why? Why did Taylor, your niece, come to you?"

"I don't think that I need to tell you anything."

"I already know it was her. She and her partner, Nancy Mosely. She wanted to get me off the volleyball team so that Gloria Delgado could have my spot and Nancy could be her backup."

"And why do you think I would care about any of that?"

"About whether Taylor's girlfriend got my spot on the team? I don't think you did care. I think you saw an opportunity to take a woman — an athletic woman—to your island boss."

"Nobody on that island was my boss."

Good. He's admitting to being on the island. I wasn't sure I could count on that.

"What made them think they could go to you to get me eliminated?"

"It didn't happen that way," he says. "It was at a family dinner, right before you all went to Manhattan for that game. Taylor just mentioned that you appeared out of nowhere and took the spot that her girlfriend was supposed to have."

I force my voice not to shake. "I see."

I'm angry. So angry, and I want to start sobbing. Sobbing for the woman I was, the woman I could've been.

But I steel myself. I won't lose it again. This may be the only chance I have to talk to Wallace.

"So you went to *her*, then."

"I did. I took her aside after dinner and asked her how badly she wanted you gone."

"And?"

"She said, 'pretty damned badly, Uncle Greg. Pretty damned badly.'"

"I'm thinking," Buck says, "that by pretty damned badly, she did not mean abducted and hunted on an island."

"I read between the lines a little." Wallace grins.

I breathe in. Exhale slowly, trying to keep my cool. "So then what?"

"I told her how to put you out of commission for the night, and then the thugs in Manhattan took you."

"So it *was* Taylor who put something in my drink on the plane."

"You're just so *smart*, Garnet."

Garnet.

The name makes me shudder.

"What was it?" I ask.

"I don't know. Something to make you puke."

"Syrup of ipecac?" Buck asks.

"No. Something worse, but I don't remember the name. This was a long time ago, you know?"

I grip the edge of the table. "Damn it, what did you give me?"

"Does it matter? You're alive. It didn't kill you."

Breathe in. Breathe out. Breathe in. Breathe out.

Don't push this, Aspen. It doesn't matter. It was over five years ago, and you're in perfect health. You've been checked out.

Don't waste the small amount of time you have on something insignificant.

"All right. So you got me out of commission, and they came and took me from my hotel room when Gloria wasn't there."

"I'm sure I don't have to tell you the rest," Wallace says. "I'm sure you remember every single detail."

"I didn't for a while," I say. "But when I did finally? The only thing I wanted was for you bastards to pay."

"Yeah? Chris Pollack gave the Feds my name."

"We know that," Buck says. "And now you have your revenge. He's going to be put away for a long time."

"Oh, he won't have to wait that long," Wallace says.

"So you have plans for him in the works," Buck says.

"Nothing I'm going to tell you about."

Buck nods.

He's okay with Pollack getting offed, and frankly, so am I. If I had my way, Wallace would get offed too.

"Why did Taylor's father cut her out of his will?" I ask.

"You'd have to ask him that."

"She's asking you, dickhead." Buck says.

"How the hell should I know? He cut me out too. Wallace Leathers was a family business. Of course he, the older son, the golden child, got everything handed to him on a silver platter."

"I'm thinking maybe he didn't go around abusing women," Buck says.

"You'd think wrong, then."

My skin goes cold.

No. Taylor's father?

"That's not true," I say. "Otherwise, he'd be behind bars just like you are."

"The golden boy? And I do mean golden boy. Beautifully golden bronze, while here I am, devoid of melanin. Genetic mutation and all that."

Something in his light eyes glimmers.

Actually glimmers, as if...

I'm not sure.

Is he telling the truth? Or is he lying?

No. Don't go there, Aspen. Don't go pulling at threads that have nothing to do with anything.

"I don't believe you," I say. "Harrison Wallace is a good man."

"Have you ever met him?"

"I think you're forgetting who's asking the questions here," Buck says.

I clear my throat. "Maybe I *will* ask him why he disowned Taylor. I have another question. Why did you guys force Taylor and Nancy to get married?"

"So they'd be in one place. Easier to keep an eye on them."

"You do know Nancy isn't gay," I say.

"Who the fuck cares?"

"All right. What else can you tell me? Anything else about how I ended up on that island?"

"That's it in a nutshell, Garnet."

"Her name is Aspen," Buck says through clenched teeth.

"She'll always be Garnet to me." He waves to a guard. "We're done over here."

37

BUCK

"You did well, baby," I say, once they take Wallace back.

She breaks down then. Sobs into my shoulder. Not giant racking sobs, but just quiet weeping.

"It's okay." I massage her back. "Everything's okay."

She pulls away and sniffles. "He's so evil. It just exudes from him, like I could almost see it coming off him in waves."

"I have a feeling he'll have a rough night tonight," Buck says.

"What do you mean?"

"Let's just say when I talked to the guard and asked if he could come back out, he made it pretty clear that they turn a blind eye to the law sometimes."

"I don't want anyone getting in trouble on my account. The guards, I mean. I don't care what happens to Wallace."

"These guys know how to cover their tracks. Do you think anybody really cares what happens to these people here? Sure, there are some people in prison who are good people who just made a bad decision. But most of them? They freaking deserve what they get."

She nods. "All right. I just don't want anyone else hurt. Except him. Except Wallace. I don't care what happens to him."

I don't either. This guy hurt the woman I love, and he deserves everything he gets. Yeah, these feelings I'm having aren't very honorable, but hell, I'm fucking human.

"Did you get the answers you wanted?" I ask.

"I suppose so. It's pretty much what I expected. You heard it all. Taylor mentioned that she wanted me out of the way, and Uncle Greg took care of it. I honestly don't believe Taylor wanted me abducted and abused."

"I doubt she wanted that either. I think she lived with that guilt for a long time, and then she was forced into marriage with a person that she didn't love and who didn't love her back. All that, and then she got disowned."

"That still bothers me," Aspen says. "Why *did* her father disinherit her? Unless he knew what a horrible thing she had done."

"Well, according to Wallace, his brother's not the saint everyone would have you believe."

"Maybe we should..."

She's not ready to give this up yet. I knew she wouldn't be. This isn't a surprise to me. She's going to want to talk to Harrison Wallace.

"He's mourning the loss of his daughter right now," I say.

"But is he? He already disowned her. If he truly knew what she did..."

"Yeah," I agree. "What Greg said doesn't make a lot of sense. If he disowned Taylor for her part in your abduction, then the logic doesn't follow. Harrison Wallace probably wasn't involved with that island."

"To be fair," Aspen says, "Greg didn't say Harrison was involved in the island. He just said that he wasn't above abusing women."

"Do we really need to find any more out?" I ask. "Taylor's dead, Aspen. She's gone. Does it matter why she was disinherited?"

"I just want the whole story, Buck. I wish there were a way to make you understand."

I do understand. I just want her to heal. I want her to move past this.

"Baby, whatever you need. If you want to talk to the senior Mr. Wallace, we will go talk to him."

"Thank you," she says. "Thank you so much, Buck."

"We're stuck here in LA until Pollack's trial anyway. We might as well give the CEO of Wallace Leathers a visit."

ONCE WE'RE in the car, Aspen pulls me to her for a searing kiss.

She's forceful—very forceful— but who am I to have a problem with that?

It's one of those raw and passionate kisses, but there's something different about this one.

Her lips, teeth, and tongue are the same, clashing with mine as we devour each other.

Something is not the same.

It's...

I can't quite put my finger on it, but it's there.

It's...unsettling.

I don't break the kiss, though. She's getting her aggressions out, and I understand. I've been there. Hell, I'm there now. Dealing with Greg Wallace affected me as well.

Not as much as it affected Aspen, but—

I hate the guy. I'd like to see him tortured, violated.

And I know what that's like.

She kisses me and kisses me and kisses me…

Until—

I finally break the kiss.

My cock is hard in my jeans, and I'm ready to pull her on top of me, grind her against me, but—

"Baby, we're in the parking lot of a prison."

"I know. Let's get in the back."

Is she serious? I eye the prison's guard tower.

"Not a good idea, Aspen."

"Then take me somewhere. Quickly, Buck. I need you. I need you inside me. Now."

It's an hour drive back to the beach house, probably nearly as far to any decent hotel.

"Baby…"

"I'm serious."

I kick the car into gear and start driving. I'm not sure where I'm going. Where do you find a place in LA that is quiet? Full of solitude?

You don't.

"Just pull over. Please."

The sedan I rented is large, but Aspen and I are tall people. We're not going to be able to have sex comfortably in the backseat.

I'm not sure she cares, though.

I keep driving.

"Buck, are you listening to me? I need you. Now."

Damn. Every time she uses the word *need*, my cock grows harder. I'm about ready to explode out of my jeans.

But her voice, the look in her eyes when I turn to regard her.

She's serious. Completely serious.

She's bordering on panic, and she knows what she needs to relax.

"All right, baby. I'll find something."

Luckily, the car has tinted windows. We can see out, but it will take someone with x-ray vision to see in.

I figured my days of having car sex were over, but this is important to her.

I pull off the highway as soon as I can and drive down the street. We pass several fast-food restaurants, and then—

A motel.

I pull into the parking lot.

Aspen grabs me and kisses me again.

I pull away. "We'll get a room."

"No. That'll take too long. It's already taken too long, Buck. Please."

Damn. "All right." I kick the car into gear once more and find a spot at the back of the parking lot, as secluded as possible. We scramble into the backseat quickly and make sure all the doors are locked.

And she's on me. On top of me, grinding against me, her lips sealed to mine.

We kiss, our tongues dueling and tangling. I breathe through my nose as best I can, but my God, my heart is beating so fast, and my breath...

I break the kiss and inhale.

She inhales as well.

She's working my belt buckle, and then my zipper, and

soon my cock is free.

Big, and aching, and free.

She scrambles out of her shorts but doesn't bother with her underwear. She simply moves it over and then—

"Oh my God!" I groan.

She's on me.

Sinking down on me, and damn... So fucking good.

She sighs then, doesn't attempt to move. Just sits on top of me, my cock embedded inside her.

Her eyes are closed, and she sighs again.

Then she leans against me, and even with our shirts on, I swear to God I can feel her. It's like her skin is against mine.

And I realize...

I need this just as much as she does.

I didn't realize how tense I was from the visit with Greg Wallace. God, especially after I found out who he truly was. I don't like wishing harm on another human being, but damn...

We're both tense, both in need of each other.

And this... Just being joined... It's enough in this moment.

I'm not sure how long we stay that way, simply joined, before she finally rises slightly and pushes herself back down on my cock.

I groan.

She groans.

She stays there again for a few moments, on top of me, our bodies joined.

And I understand. I understand why she needs this.

But I have a need as well. I need to fuck.

So I lift her hips. I take control. I move her up to the tip of my dick, let her labia tickle the head, and then I push her back down.

I groan.

She groans.

And I do it again.

I take control.

At first I thought she needed to be in control. This was all her idea after all.

But now? I see what she truly needs.

She needs *me*. She needs me to give her what she desires.

And I'm all too happy to do so.

I go slowly at first, holding her on the tip of my cock for a few seconds before slamming her back down.

Then I increase the tempo, and finally she joins in, moving up and down of her own accord. I still grip her hips.

She slides one hand under the waistband of her panties, and damn...

When she touches herself I go fucking crazy.

I won't last much longer, but I want her to have the orgasm she so desperately needs.

So I brace myself, hold myself in check, until—

"Ahhh!" Her shoulders shudder.

The contractions of her walls, those sweet vibrations... I feel every one against my sensitive dick.

That's my signal.

I push my hips upward, jam myself into her, and I release.

Our groans intermingle, until I'm not sure which are coming from me and which from her. All I know is that I'm emptying into her, releasing, and a wave of calm settles over me.

A wave of calm we both need.

We stay joined for a few moments, until Aspen finally pulls away from me. I look out the window of the car.

People walk by, coming and going, but nothing looks out

of place.

Not that it matters.

This was going to happen whether we were putting ourselves on display or not.

I'm not an exhibitionist, and I don't think Aspen is either. Plus, I sure as hell don't want to be arrested.

No harm done.

The tinted windows did their job.

I reach in my pocket, but I don't have a handkerchief or bandanna. Not something I normally carry. But I need to give Aspen something to help her clean up.

"Baby..."

"It's okay," she says. "I have tissues in my purse." But her purse is in the front seat.

"I'll get it for you." I strap my cock back into my jeans, open the door, get into the driver's seat, find her purse, and hand it back to her.

"Thanks," she says.

A few moments later she joins me in the front seat.

"That was pretty awesome," I say.

"It was awesome, yes, but it was also necessary, Buck. I can't tell you how much I needed it."

"I needed it too, baby. We both did. This day has been trying, to say the least."

"It was. I can't believe he's the one..." She trails her hand absently over her right breast.

"He'll pay for that, baby."

"He's already paying for it," she says. "Please. Please don't put yourself in any danger."

"I won't."

And it's true. I won't. But I will see that Greg Wallace is taken care of one way or another.

38

ASPEN

Getting in to see Harrison Wallace turns out to be harder than I expected it to be.

In the end, Luke's father is the one who makes it happen.

They've done business in the past, although what kind of business a B-movie producer has with a leather magnate is beyond me. However, we can't get in to see him for a couple of weeks.

So we decide on a different plan of action.

Taylor's funeral.

Whether Harrison will show up, we have no idea. He did disown her after all. But death has a way of bringing people together, usually after it's too late.

Katelyn and I went shopping yesterday to purchase black dresses.

Now, we're en route to the funeral.

We arrive at the small church and walk inside.

Taylor was cremated, and an urn of her ashes sits at the altar, along with a picture of her and Nancy.

Nancy, of course, isn't here. She's in prison.

"That must be the family up in that front row," Katelyn says to me.

"I've seen pictures of her father," I say. "If he turned around, I could tell if it's him."

"It's him," Buck says. "Luke and I made sure he'd be here."

"Good. I'll talk to him when we go through the receiving line."

"Are you sure, baby? This is his daughter's funeral. We should be respectful."

"I get that, but obviously there was not a lot of love lost there. He disowned her. He probably shouldn't even be here."

"Of course he should be here," Buck says. "He's her father. He's probably paying for everything. This is a pretty nice sendoff."

"You think he's paying for the funeral of the daughter he disowned?"

"Who else would pay for it? Not Nancy. She's in jail. Plus, she was a wife in name only."

"Do you think any of these people are wondering why Taylor's wife isn't here?"

"I don't know—" Buck stops when the minister walks to the pulpit.

"Thank you all for coming today," he says. "We're here to mourn the loss of Taylor Helaine Wallace. Harry, Rita, Jocelyn, Gary, we're all so sorry for your loss. If you will all please rise, we'll begin with our opening hymn."

The organist begins playing, and I turn to the requisite page in the hymnal sitting in front of me.

But I don't sing.

I simply mouth the words.

I'm not here to mourn.

I'm here to find answers.

AN HOUR LONG. The service was an hour long. Harrison Wallace and his wife didn't speak, but Taylor's brother and sister did. So did several others. It was never-ending.

Buck joins me in the receiving line. Luke and Katelyn chose to skip it.

First in line is Taylor's sister, Jocelyn.

"I'm so very sorry for your loss," I say to her, holding out my hand.

"Thank you very much. How did you know Taylor?"

"We played professional volleyball together. My name is Aspen Davis."

Jocelyn's eyes widen. "You're Aspen Davis?"

"I am."

"But we all thought you were—"

"I assure you I'm alive and well. This is my boyfriend, Buck Moreno."

Jocelyn shakes Buck's hand, and then she introduces us to her brother standing next to her. "Gary, this is Aspen Davis, and her boyfriend."

Gary, who looks exactly like Taylor in male form, drops his jaw. "Aspen Davis?"

"Yes, reports of my demise were false."

"Oh, I didn't mean—"

I shake my head. "It's okay. I'm very sorry for your loss, Gary."

"Thank you. And thank you both for coming."

Taylor's mother is next. I shake her hand. "I'm very sorry for your loss, Mrs. Wallace."

She simply nods, her eyes glazed over with tears.

And next... Harrison Wallace. He's a nice-looking older man, hardly gray at all.

I hold out my hand. "Mr. Wallace, I'm Aspen Davis. I played volleyball with your daughter. I'm very sorry for your loss."

Harrison Wallace lifts his eyebrows. "Did you say Aspen Davis?"

"Yes, and I know this is your daughter's funeral, but I really would like to speak to you if possible."

He cocks his head and stops the handshake. "As you said, this is my daughter's funeral."

"I understand, and I do respect that."

He doesn't let my hand go, though. He holds onto it, and then he seems to look deep into my eyes. "I will speak with you. When I'm done here in the receiving line and before I head to the wake."

"You will? That means so much to me. Thank you so much."

"Wait for me outside the church in the back. I will be there."

Buck and I leave the receiving line, and we confer quickly with Luke and Katelyn. While Buck and I wait outside behind the church, Luke and Katelyn station themselves in the front, just in case Harrison Wallace was lying and has no intention of speaking to us.

But after fifteen minutes, Harrison comes out the back of the church and nods to us, pointing and gesturing us to follow him.

We end up in a secluded gazebo, where we're able to speak freely.

"We weren't sure you were going to show," Buck says.

"To be honest," Harrison says, "I wasn't sure I was going to either. But if you have questions, Ms. Davis, I feel it's my duty to answer them to the best of my ability."

"Call me Aspen," I say, "and thank you. You have no idea how much this means to me."

"I'm not certain that I will have any of the answers you're looking for, but I will try."

I clear my throat. "I know who's responsible for my...elimination."

"I'm so glad you're okay," he says. "What happened to you?"

"I'm sure you probably already know. I was abducted and taken to Derek Wolfe's island in the South Pacific. I was hunted. Violated. For a period of over five years."

He shakes his head. "My God. I'm so sorry."

"Can we assume you had nothing to do with this?" Buck says.

"I can see why you might think I would have, but I didn't. I had no idea what my brother was up to. It's difficult to say this about a person you grew up with, but he got what was coming to him."

"We know," I say. "We spoke with him a few days ago."

His eyebrows fly up. "You spoke to Greg?"

"We did."

"That's impossible."

"Why would you say that?"

"Because Greg was killed in prison over a week ago."

39

BUCK

No. Just no. This story can't get any creepier.

"No, he wasn't," I say. "We spoke with him."

"Then you spoke to an imposter."

"Your brother's an albino, right?" I say.

Wallace raises his eyebrows. "An albino? Hell, no. He had the same complexion I have. Naturally tan."

Aspen's lips form an O. "I don't understand. The man I saw —the man they brought to me who they said was Greg Wallace —is an albino. Pasty white skin and blue eyes. White hair. He knew the whole story. Said Taylor came to him and— Oh my God. And the albino... He tormented me on that island."

"I'm very sorry you were tormented, my dear, but that man was not my brother."

"Who the hell was he then?" I ask.

"If I knew, I would tell you."

"We're going to need a lot more information," Aspen says. "I'm sorry about your daughter, Mr. Wallace, but—"

"You don't have to be sorry about my daughter, Ms. Davis.

I know what she did to you. What she and Nancy and Greg did to you. There's no excuse for it, and there's no way I can make it up to you. Although I would if I could."

"You knew," I say.

Harrison Wallace doesn't reply at first.

"Maybe you didn't know what was going to happen to Aspen, but you knew what your brother was doing."

"I did not condone it."

"But you knew." I inch closer to Wallace. "You knew what they were doing to these young women. How could you not say anything?"

"Gentlemen's agreement." Wallace shifts from one foot to another. "Most men above a certain paygrade were aware of what was going on at Derek Wolfe's island. Epstein's island. We all knew. Anyone who could afford to go knew."

"And yet... you did nothing?" I say.

"It's not that simple. These are powerful people. People who tend to"—air quote—"*take care* of anyone who interferes."

I shake my head. "Sometimes I hate humanity."

"Mr. Moreno," Wallace says, "sometimes I do too. Do you think it was easy for me to disown my daughter? My brother?"

"Your brother had his own money."

"He did. Although a lot less of it once I cut him off."

"Yet enough to keep going to the island," Aspen says.

"Actually, from what I understand, it cost over a million dollars a day to be on that island. Once I disowned him, he no longer went there."

"So he couldn't have been the one who tormented me." Aspen shakes her head.

"You're right. Because once I found out what Greg helped Taylor do, I disowned both of them."

"But Greg's name was still on the master list," Buck says.

"That's right. And apparently there was a narc who named him as well."

"Pollack," I say.

"Is that his name?"

"It's the name he's using, and yes, he's in jail awaiting trial for two counts of murder. And I'm guessing, now that his immunity is revoked, a bunch of other crimes as well."

Wallace's eyes widen. "You think he killed my brother in prison?"

"I think he probably had something to do with it. I doubt he could actually get into the prison and take care of your brother."

"So some jackass narc, who turned on my brother in the first place, had him killed?"

"It's my fault," Aspen says. "I started asking questions."

I grab Aspen's hand. "Baby, none of this is your fault."

"No, it's not." Wallace shakes his head. "It would be easy for me to blame you, Ms. Davis. You were there when my daughter took her own life. And she took her life because you were there asking questions. But is it your fault? No. It's not. You have the right to answers. And what my daughter did… I'll never understand, and I've thought about it *ad nauseum*. For the last five years, ever since I found out and disowned her."

"Some people…" I say.

"You must think I was a terrible parent. But Rita and I… Rita never got over this. And now, Taylor is gone forever. Jocelyn and Gary? They don't know either. They don't understand any of it."

"Why did you force Taylor to marry Nancy?" Aspen asks.

"That wasn't me. That was Greg's idea. He figured it was better to keep them both close."

"Nancy claims she's not gay," I say.

"I don't think she is. It didn't really matter. It was purely a marriage of convenience. To keep Nancy and Taylor close so Greg could keep an eye on them."

"What did Greg do after he no longer had money to go to the island?" I ask.

"He had a nest egg of his own. For a while he got involved in drugs."

"Oh my God. Did he happen to know a kingpin named Lucifer Raven?"

"I don't know. I disowned him. I have no idea what he was into."

Luke. Raven. Somehow I just know he's involved in this.

More than he's told me so far.

Hey, I get it. He wants to start a new life with Katelyn.

I had pledged to stay out of his way, but...

If he has information about Greg Wallace and how this all came about, I want it.

"I really should get to the wake," Wallace says.

"We've got an appointment with you in a couple of weeks," Aspen says. "It was the best we could do. But if possible, we'd like to talk to you more. Soon."

He nods. Pulls a card out of his pocket. "Call this number. Tell them you need to see me tomorrow. I'll make sure you get on the calendar."

"Thank you," Aspen says.

"Will you be coming to the wake?"

"No," I say.

"I understand. I'll talk to both of you tomorrow."

40

ASPEN

Buck is angry.

Luke and Katelyn went ahead home after the funeral.

But now...

Buck wants to know more.

As soon as Harrison Wallace mentioned that his brother got into the drug business, I knew Buck was going to go for Luke's jugular.

"Calm down," I say as we drive back to the beach house.

"Calm down? Fucking Raven probably knows more than he's letting on."

"I don't think so, Buck. He loves Katelyn, and Katelyn loves me. If he had any more information, he'd tell us."

"Yeah? I will find out everything he knows if I have to beat it out of him."

I bite my lower lip. How can I reason with Buck? All this time, he's tried to get me to back down. To simply focus on healing rather than dredging up the past.

I couldn't do it.

Seems the tides have turned now.

"Luke wasn't Luke then, Buck. You know it and I know it."

"Right. He was the guy who abused my sister, kept her locked in the very damned house we're staying at."

"I know. But that's not who he is anymore, and Emily is happy. You said so yourself."

"She is."

"And so are you. We found each other. Just like Emily found Scotty. And Katelyn..."

"You know I adore Katelyn," Buck says, "but for God's sake. She can do better."

"Not in her eyes she can't. She and Luke are in love. You can feel it every time the two of them are together. They don't take their eyes off each other, and they're always touching in some small way. She's happy, Buck, and I don't want to take that away from her."

He inhales, holds it for moment, and then exhales with a whoosh. "Don't you want all the answers, Aspen? Isn't that what you've been gunning for this whole time?"

"I know. But not if it's going to hurt Katelyn."

"For crying out loud, you were fine if *you* were the one getting hurt."

"I suppose I was," I say. "But maybe I was wrong, Buck. I dragged you into all of this. You, the man I love more than anything. I shouldn't have done that. You got hurt."

"I'm fine."

"Yeah, you're fine. Because Luke went to find you. You might've bled out on Gloria's carpet otherwise."

He stiffens a moment.

Good. He's thinking.

"I still want to know what he knows."

"Fine. I want to know as well. But don't hurt him. For me. For Katelyn."

He doesn't respond.

And just when I think he's never going to respond—

"Fine." His lips are pursed into a line.

And that's quite a feat for someone with beautiful full lips like Buck Moreno.

"I DON'T KNOW what you're talking about," Luke says.

We're back at the beach house and out on the deck having a glass of wine—Luke's having sparkling water.

Buck shakes his head. "Funny that I don't believe you."

"The underground drug trade is huge in LA," Luke says. "I had never heard of Greg Wallace before I met Aspen, and I don't know him by any other name either. Don't you think I care about these women just as much as you do?"

Buck doesn't respond.

"Buck..." From Katelyn.

"Don't," Luke says. "He's never going to forgive me for what I put his sister through. And frankly? I don't even blame him."

"I think he's telling the truth, Buck," I say. "He's been researching this thing using all his connections. If he had come across Greg Wallace, he would've told us."

Luke nods. "Absolutely."

"Fine. Whatever." Buck takes a sip of his wine. "You got any bourbon?"

"Of course he doesn't have any bourbon," I say.

"Actually," Katelyn says, "we do have some bourbon. We keep a stocked bar, you know, for guests."

Buck rises. "Just show me the way."

He returns a few moments later with a couple fingers full of bourbon, neat. He downs it all in one swallow.

"Smooth," he says. "Nothing but the best for you, huh, Raven?"

Luke doesn't reply.

In my estimation, Luke is being very patient with Buck.

And Buck is being...

He's being a brother. And I understand.

"Fine," Buck finally says. "So you didn't know Greg Wallace when you were into drugs."

"First of all, I wasn't into drugs. I *sold* drugs. I was into alcohol."

"Whatever."

"And no, I did *not* know Greg Wallace. I could put out some feelers, if you want, but I'm not sure why it would matter at this point. The man is clearly dead."

"Yeah, but why did the albino take his place? They obviously knew each other from the island."

"I guess we need to figure out who the albino truly is," Katelyn says, "and what his connection is."

"I know what his connection is," I say dryly.

Buck tenses next to me. "It's okay, baby."

"Katelyn knows everything."

"Oh, Aspen," Katelyn says. "He's not the one..."

I simply nod.

"I'm so sorry. I'm so sorry you had to face him."

"I'm not. It was hard. No doubt. But I feel better. It's kind of like eating those fish tacos, just a million times more difficult. But I feel like a got a little piece of myself back."

"Piece by piece, baby," Buck says. "That's how you've got to take it. You will come back. Hell, you're already back."

"You understand, don't you?"

"Hell yeah. There are parts of me that are still in Afghanistan. But little by little, I'm getting them all back. You've helped a lot with that."

I take his hand and squeeze it.

I look at Buck, and then at Luke.

Katelyn is the closest thing I have to a best friend. I love her dearly, and it would be so great if Luke and Buck could be friends as well.

I think Luke would be up for it. But Buck?

I'm not sure he ever will be. Not that I can blame him.

I mean, I don't have any siblings, but if I did, how could I forgive someone who hurt one of them? I could never forgive anyone who hurt Buck or Katelyn.

So I'll be more patient. More understanding.

"All right," I say. "A couple of things. Chris Pollack."

"What about him?" Katelyn says.

"He's probably the one who offed Greg Wallace. I mean, it happened right around the time Gloria and Brian were killed."

"But why?" Luke asks. "Wallace was already in prison."

"Yeah, but he knew stuff. And since he was already in prison, there was no reason for him not to speak up."

"But it doesn't make sense," Luke says. "He knew way more than Gloria and Brian knew."

"Right," I say.

"I have to admit I'm baffled." From Buck.

It's a mystery...and I want to know the answers. But is it time to let this go?

I know how I got on that island now. The people responsible are paying or have paid for it.

Maybe there are some things I just don't need to know.

"Maybe it's time we move on," I say to Buck. "We can find a place of our own. Settle down."

"Here?" Buck says.

"I know it's probably not your first choice," I say. "But Katelyn is the closest thing I have to a sister, a best friend, and I think we need to be near each other."

"I second that," Katelyn says.

"But your family's in Colorado," Buck says. "And the Wolfes..."

"You can work for the Wolfes from here," I say. "And I know they're good people. I get it. But I can't be close to the Wolfes, Buck. Their father is the one who..."

He squeezes my hand this time. "I understand, baby. It's too much for you."

"That's just it. It's not that it's too much for me. It's just that I need to take back my life. And I think I want to start here."

"We can't afford a place like this." Buck rolls his eyes.

"Are you kidding me? I don't care where we live, Buck. We can live in a one-room apartment. A shack. As long as we're together."

41

BUCK

We sit in the reception area of the Wallace Leathers corporate headquarters.

True to his word, Harrison Wallace made time for us today. He's willing to answer more questions.

Something needles at the back of my neck, though. Call it my fight-or-flight instinct.

I'm not sure why, but I feel like we're walking into something.

Another one of my hunches.

And I can't ignore it.

Aspen has more questions for this man, but I'm not sure he'll be able to answer any of them. Does he even know who the albino is?

And why the albino took his brother's place?

We won't find those answers here.

Harrison Wallace himself comes out to greet us. "Mr. Moreno and Ms. Davis. Thank you for coming in. Come on back."

We rise. Aspen sets down the coffee table book she was

perusing. I eye the title. *Disneyland Through the Years*. I can't help a slight smile. She truly is a Disney princess with those big brown eyes and long lashes.

She can deny it all she wants, but it's true.

We follow Harrison back to his corner office. Glass windows line both outer walls, and the view is spectacular.

"Have a seat, both of you."

He walks behind his desk, and Aspen and I sit in the lush leather chairs facing him.

"I'm sorry I didn't have more time to talk to you yesterday."

"We totally understand, Mr. Wallace," Aspen says. "It was your daughter's funeral, after all."

"Yes, it was. But unfortunately, Rita and I had to say goodbye to Taylor a long time ago. After what she did to you."

"But she's still your daughter," I say.

"Was," he says. "She's in a better place now, Mr. Moreno."

"Buck."

"Then you must call me Harry." He turns to Aspen. "Now Ms. Davis, what else can I enlighten you on?"

Aspen clears her throat. "I guess I just want to know... why? What made Taylor go rogue like that? At the time, she was dating my backup, Gloria Delgado, and Nancy was third in line for my position."

"I don't think she ever really got over Gloria," Harrison says. "She used to call Gloria the love of her life."

"Really?" Aspen says.

"Yes. I think she was more upset than Gloria was when you took the spot on the team."

Aspen wrinkles her forehead.

That doesn't jibe with what Gloria or Taylor told us.

But then again, why should we believe Taylor? After all, she's the one who got this whole ball rolling.

"According to Taylor and Nancy," I say, "Gloria was very upset about Aspen taking her place on the team. And she was upset that she was reacting negatively, as she was a devout Catholic and didn't like having these kinds of feelings about someone."

"She was a devout Catholic?"

"Oh, yes," Aspen says. "Very. Very nice girl, and she prayed for everyone."

"That's strange," Harrison says. "Taylor never mentioned that."

"She didn't mention that her girlfriend was a devout Catholic?" I ask.

"Not that I recall. I think I would've remembered that."

"Yeah, you probably would have," Aspen says.

"Well, I suppose it doesn't matter now," Wallace says. "They're both gone."

"Yes." I clear my throat. "They are."

Something is not right here.

Then again, windows line this entire office. Anyone can see what goes on in here. At least anyone who can see up to the fortieth floor.

"We need to find out who this albino is," I say. "He's the one who truly tormented Aspen on that island. He caused her much distress and injury."

"I wish I could help you. I don't understand the workings of the prison system. I would imagine anyone who tried to take my brother's place had to have help from the inside."

"From guards, yes," I say.

"Are you absolutely sure it was your brother who was killed?" Aspen asks.

"I identified the body myself," Wallace says. "And he was cremated."

"And this happened a week ago?"

"Yes. I saw no reason to have any kind of memorial for him. The man was a degenerate."

"I see your point," I say.

"How do we find out who the albino is?" Aspen asks.

"You'd need some help on the inside," Wallace says. "And I don't have that for you. I'm sorry."

"I understand." I rise.

"I'm sorry I couldn't be more help."

Aspen rises then. "Thank you for seeing us. I guess we ought to go."

Wallace stands. "All right. You have my number if you need anything else."

I turn toward the door, but then I look over my shoulder. "I just have one more question for you, Harrison."

"Certainly. Whatever I can do to help."

I don't have a question. Just a hunch. Just a feeling that we don't have all the information.

And then, on his credenza behind him, I see it.

42

ASPEN

I'm not sure what more Buck thinks he can ask Mr. Wallace. He clearly doesn't know who the albino is. And maybe it's okay that I don't know. He's in prison. He's not getting out anytime soon, except...

If he had enough connections in prison to take the place of Greg Wallace...

My God.

I'm still not safe from him.

A bizarre look passes between Buck and Mr. Wallace.

I cock my head, not sure what—

Then I gasp.

In a flash, they're both armed, guns pointing at each other.

"Buck!"

"Get out of here, Aspen. Now," he says, his voice not wavering.

My heart begins to pound. "No, no, I'm not leaving you."

"You might want to do what he says, Missy." From Wallace.

"Please," Buck says between clenched teeth. "Leave."

But my feet are glued to the fucking floor.

I can't leave. I can't leave Buck.

"What's going on? I don't understand. We're all on the same side here."

"That's where you're wrong, Missy." Harrison shakes his head and glares at Buck. "What do you think you have on me?"

"The conch shell on your credenza behind your desk. It's a milk conch. My sister has one just like it."

"It's a trinket," Wallace says. "Maybe I picked it up in a thrift shop near Venice Beach."

"Nice try," Buck says. "First, I doubt you'd ever go within a hundred yards of a thrift shop, but that's neither here nor there. I happen to know that thick shells like that are only found in the deepest parts of the Southwest Pacific Ocean. And I happen to know of an island where they're abundant."

"Maybe my brother gave it to me."

"Maybe. But I'm thinking if he did, you wouldn't be holding a gun on me right now."

I gasp.

"Please," Buck says, "leave, Aspen."

But my feet don't want to move.

I can't leave Buck.

Buck, who has become everything to me.

"You want to tell the story now?" Buck says. "Or after I shoot you in the shoulder?"

"Have you forgotten I'm holding a gun as well?"

"Yeah, but I'm thinking I'm probably a better shot. I used to be a sniper."

Within a flash, Wallace's arm moves, and the gun is pointing at me.

"How about now? You willing to take a chance?"

I gasp, fear racing through me and making my blood curdle in my veins.

My stomach lurches, and I think I'm going to puke. Or soil myself. Probably both.

This fear, this fear...

This is something Buck knows, and my God...

I've been through the worst hell someone can imagine, but at least I lived.

And I may not live now.

"Buck," I say, my voice shaking, "I don't understand what's going on here."

I'm armed, of course. My gun is strapped to my shoulder underneath my T-shirt.

I can't get it without moving, and Wallace will shoot me dead before I can get hold of it.

Why didn't I leave when Buck told me to?

I went through all that hell on the island, over five years, and now I'm healing, and I found someone who I want to spend my life with.

But now my life may be over.

It's not fair. It's just not fair.

"Care to explain?" Buck says.

"Not particularly."

"Let her go," Buck says. "This is between the two of us."

"I'm afraid I can't let her go." He turns to me. "You should've escaped when you had the chance, Missy. But now, I'm afraid I'm going to have to take you both out."

"Why?" I cry. "I don't understand."

"If I had to guess," Buck says, his voice never wavering, "I'd say the albino wasn't lying about the elder Wallace, and that *Harry* here is the one who actually went to that island.

The one who abused and tortured you girls. And then he framed his brother for it."

"You know you can't know all of this and live," Wallace says.

"If I die, you die."

"What about your lady here?"

Buck stiffens. "Let her go. And then you and I can have it out. Last man standing."

"I'm afraid I can't let either one of you out of here alive." Still training the gun on me, he reaches into his top drawer and screws on a silencer. "Tell you what we're going to do. I just had my office redecorated, and I really don't want blood all over it. So we're going to walk out of here, slowly, as if nothing's wrong."

"And you really think I'm going to let you do that?"

He cocks the trigger. "Yeah, I think you will, or I kill your girlfriend."

43

BUCK

I must stay strong.

I must protect Aspen.

Damn, I should've gone with my instinct.

I should've never come here, or at the very least I should've never brought Aspen here.

Why didn't I follow my hunch?

If something happens to her...

How can I live with that?

I've been through hell. I've been tortured, violated, shot, stabbed.

None of it broke me, though it came close.

Losing Aspen? That will break me.

I won't recover.

If he's going to shoot Aspen, he may as well shoot me.

But I can't let it happen.

Aspen must live. If I have to die, so be it. But Aspen *must live*.

If the gun were still pointed at me, I would take the shot.

The shot to his shoulder, and I would take the chance of him killing me.

But while the gun is pointing at Aspen?

I absolutely cannot take that chance.

I'm not sure how Wallace thinks he's going to get us out of here, with his entire staff right outside the door. He'll find a way though. Clearly this isn't the first time he's been in this situation.

"It was you," Aspen says quietly, her voice soft and shaking. "It was you, not your brother. Taylor went to *you*."

"Well, I *am* her father."

"Why disown her then? Why? When you're the one who—"

"Quiet!"

Aspen shuts her mouth and visibly shudders.

"This is between you and me," I say to Wallace through clenched teeth, steeling myself. "Let. Her. Go."

"And I've told you before. This is all about her. She's the one who set all of this in motion."

"No, *you're* the one who set all of this in motion. You're the one who put her on that island. And why? So your daughter's girlfriend could have her spot on the team? And then you disown your own daughter? What aren't you telling me?"

"You really think I'm going to answer any more questions?" He's cold as ice. "I've got my gun on your girlfriend here. And believe me, I'm not a novice at this."

I believe him. But for every trigger he's pulled, I'm pretty sure I've pulled about a hundred.

I need to distract him in some way. Distract him so Aspen can either get her gun or get out of here.

And I hope it's the latter. If she has to shoot a person...

It's hard to recover from that, even when the person has it coming.

Wallace's phone buzzes.

Saved by the bell? I'm not sure. He could easily ignore it.

So I'm surprised when he doesn't. He taps it with his free hand. "Yes, Denise?"

"Mr. Wallace? There's someone here to see you, and he's being very insistent."

"He'll have to wait. I'm in a very important meeting."

"Yes, I've told him that, but—"

"That's all, Denise." He flips off the intercom.

All right. Not bad. His voice is as icy as ever, but he didn't give anything away. Except for the fact that he didn't want to be bothered in this meeting. He wasn't even interested in hearing who needed to see him so urgently.

Which means... Hell, I don't know what it means.

"Please," I say.

Yes, I'm going to resort to begging.

"Please, just let her go."

"Not happening. Not today."

I've been in this situation before.

But the person on the other end of the gun was never Aspen. Never my forever love, the love of my life. The woman who's been through so much already. Her life can't end like this.

It just can't.

Think, Buck. For God's sake, think!

How can I distract him?

I train my gun on his shoulder.

I hold steady.

Then, with my peripheral vision, I glance around the

room, looking for something—anything—that I can use as a distraction.

What is his weakness?

He's a psychopath, so he probably doesn't have one. He doesn't have a conscience. He didn't care about his daughter because he disinherited her. At first we thought he disinherited her because she went to her uncle and had Aspen abducted, but that's not the case. Did he even have a reason to cut her off? Does he care about his wife? His other two children? Doubtful.

He certainly didn't care about his brother because he framed him. *And* had him killed.

The albino?

He claims not to know who the albino is.

But perhaps that's the key.

"Put the gun down, Wallace," I say. "I need to get my phone."

"Right. I'm not about to let you call the cops. Are you that naïve?"

"Not naïve at all. But I do need to make a call. Because in the next half an hour, both the albino and Chris Pollack are going to be killed. It's already set."

"And you think I care about that?"

All right. Apparently not. He doesn't care about either of those people, so no leverage there.

"Yes, they will both be offed, and only they have information that could exonerate you."

Wallace wrinkles his forehead, cocks his head.

Peripherally I look at Aspen. *Don't move*, I tell her in my mind. *I know you're thinking about going for your weapon, but don't move. It's too dangerous.*

She stiffens.

Good. I may not have gotten through to her clairvoyantly, but she came to the same conclusion.

Sweat begins to emerge on Wallace's forehead.

Interesting. Up until now, he was cool as a fucking alley cat.

All right. My mention of Pollack and the albino got to him.

There's something there after all.

"I can still call it off," I say.

He doesn't respond. But his hand shakes.

Just a bit, but it shakes.

And that's my window of opportunity.

In less than a second, I retrain my target onto his wrist. I shoot, and he goes down while his gun clatters to the floor.

Aspen shrieks.

I grab her and push her out the door, right into Luke's arms.

"What are you doing here?" I demand.

"Trying to save your damned ass."

"Call the fucking cops, will you? I need to get back in there and—"

I race back into the room. Someone needs to be watching Wallace.

But somehow, he's crawled to his gun, picked it up in his other hand.

A left-handed shot? That could get messy.

He pulls the gun on me.

"No way. No fucking way."

He cocks it.

Then a gunshot.

I clench my teeth, grit against the pain, the blood...

Except...it doesn't come.

No one shot me.

Aspen. God, not Aspen! "Baby! Are you okay?"

She runs to me, and only then do I notice Harrison Wallace in a heap on the floor.

The shot came from Luke, behind me.

"Call 911," Luke says. "Gunshot to the wrist and to the shoulder. This degenerate has to live."

44

ASPEN

Harrison Wallace is only alive because both Buck and Luke are such great shots.

"He can't die," Luke says, as the paramedics roll him out on the stretcher.

"We'll do everything we can for him, sir," one of them says.

"I don't think you understand." This time Buck speaks. "According to my friend here, this man has information that we need. Information about two murders and a suicide. An assault and battery. Make that two assaults. He was just holding my girlfriend at gunpoint."

"Our job is to keep him alive until we get to the hospital, sir," another paramedic says. "It doesn't matter to us what he's accused of or what information he has. We just need to do the best we can to keep him alive."

Buck nods. "Good enough." Then he turns to Luke. "We need to talk."

"We do. But we're following him to the hospital. We're not letting that motherfucker out of our sight."

~

THE THREE OF us are in the ER waiting room at Sinai, the same hospital they took Buck to after his head wound.

I'm nervous. Shaking and nervous. Not because I care about Harrison Wallace's life. I don't. Because, according to Luke, he has information that we need.

"He tried to hide it," Buck says, "but when I mentioned Chris Pollack and the albino, I could tell it got to him."

"That's the reason I came," Luke says. "One of my contacts came in with some very interesting information about Harrison Wallace, Chris Pollack, and a man named Fernando Smith."

"Let me guess. Fernando Smith is an albino."

"You got it."

I listen, clasping my hands together, trying not to shiver. It seems like every air conditioner in LA is set to fifty degrees. I get that LA is hot, but really?

Besides, I know I'm not shivering because of the air conditioning. I'm shivering because...

Only moments ago, a gun was pointed at me.

Only moments ago, both Buck and Luke shot Harrison Wallace.

I'm a good shot. I learned from my father, and he's the best. But I wouldn't have been able to make either of those shots, not in this lifetime.

Buck was a sniper, so it makes sense that he could make a shot like that. But Luke? I suppose you learn to defend yourself very well when you're in the underground drug trade. Also when your father has a shooting range in his basement bunker.

A woman rushes in.

I recognize her at once from the funeral. This is Rita Wallace, Harrison's wife and Taylor's mother. She looks exactly like Taylor, except that she's about twenty years older and without the blue hair. She's dressed to the nines, of course, dripping in diamonds with a rock the size of Texas on her left hand.

"I'm looking for my husband," she says to the clerk at the reception desk. "Harrison Wallace. Apparently he's been shot?"

"Yes ma'am," the receptionist tells her. "His doctor should be out soon to talk to you. In the meantime you can join his friends over there." The reception clerk gestures to us.

She looks toward us and wrinkles her forehead. "I don't know any of those people."

She looks at me, and then to Buck, and then back again. Then she walks toward us.

"I saw you two at Taylor's funeral."

Buck clears his throat. "Yes, ma'am, you did."

"Friends of Taylor's from volleyball?"

I nod then. "Yes. I'm Aspen Davis."

"Why are you here? How did you find out about Harry being shot?"

"That's a long story, ma'am." From Buck.

She rubs at her temples with a shaking hand. "I can't be bothered with that now. I need to find out if he's okay. Have you heard anything?"

"They won't give us any information," Luke says. "Only family. Now that you're here, maybe some of them will speak to you."

"He was shot? Twice?"

"He was," Buck says. "In the wrist and the shoulder. They shouldn't be life-threatening wounds."

"How do you know where he was shot?"

Neither Luke nor Buck says a word.

The silence becomes interminable.

"We were there, ma'am," Buck finally says.

"You were there? At his office? How did this happen?"

"I think you'll need to talk to the police about that," Buck says.

"The police? What are you talking about? Who shot my husband?"

Luke opens his mouth, but a doctor dressed in blue scrubs comes out through double doors.

"I'm looking for Mrs. Harrison Walker," she says.

Mrs. Wallace stands. "You mean Mrs. Harrison Wallace?"

"Right. I'm sorry."

"I'm Rita Wallace."

The doctor holds out her hand. "I'm Dr. Duluth, the resident on your husband's case. He's going to need surgery on his wrist. The gunshot wound shattered it."

Mrs. Wallace gulps. "But is he okay? Will he live?"

"Yes, ma'am. At this point we expect him to make a full recovery. Though he may have limited movement in his wrist."

"What about the other wound? The shoulder?"

"The bullet went through. No major blood vessels were affected. We've already stitched up the wound and gotten him started on antibiotics."

Mrs. Wallace sits down in a chair and sighs. "Thank God."

"I'm happy we could give you some good news," Dr. Duluth says. "I need to return and prep for surgery. Either I or the attending surgeon will be out to give you an update when he's finished."

"Yes, Doctor. Thank you."

Dr. Duluth nods. "You're very welcome." Then she moves swiftly across the waiting area and back through the double doors.

Mrs. Wallace sits with her head in her hands as two police officers walk toward her.

I almost feel bad for her.

Almost.

She may well be innocent in all of this. Who knows? But is she truly innocent? If she were, wouldn't her daughter have been a better person?

Her husband probably kept his X-rated escapades from her, but Taylor?

None of it makes sense.

We can't really talk, with Mrs. Wallace sitting so close to us.

Buck stands then. "Mrs. Wallace, we're very happy to hear that your husband will be okay." Then to Luke and me. "We should go."

I know what he means. He's not suggesting that we leave the hospital. But we need to leave this area, so we can speak freely.

"Yes, of course," Mrs. Wallace says. "Thank you for being here with him."

Buck merely nods, and Luke and I don't say anything as we walk out of the waiting area.

Once outside—

Luke turns to Buck. "Let's go somewhere secure."

"Back to your place?" Buck says.

He nods. "Wallace is under guard, so he's not going anywhere. Katelyn will be worried, and I don't want her to go through any pain."

"We'll see you there."

45

BUCK

Aspen and I are quiet as we drive to the beach house, following Luke in his Tesla.

I don't speak because I can't put one thought out of my mind: If not for Luke Ashton — Lucifer Raven—I could be dead right now.

Most likely not, as the chance of Harrison Wallace making a left-handed shot wasn't good, but what if he'd been able to?

Even a bad shot could have done significant damage.

Now I'm indebted to Luke.

I don't like the feeling.

But he didn't have to take the shot.

Now he's going to have to answer to the cops, and he may well lose his immunity. Or at least go on probation or something. I can't imagine any immunity agreement that allows him to be in possession of a firearm.

He fucking saved me.

And boy, that grates on me.

Aspen lets out a soft sigh.

"You okay, baby?"

"I'm so far from okay, Buck. But at least we're getting some answers. Harrison Wallace almost evaded us."

"I know."

"If you hadn't recognized that conch shell..."

"Even with the conch shell, it was still a long shot. I mean, maybe he just collects shells from South Pacific places. But I just had a feeling when we walked in that office. The hair on the back of my neck stood up. I knew something was off."

"Your instinct is phenomenal," she says. "I owe you everything, Buck."

"I wish my instinct had kicked in a little sooner, before I took you in there."

"You think you could have kept me out?" She rubs my thigh. "I'm fine. We're both fine. You saved me. You got that shot to his wrist and got his gun off me."

I say nothing.

Yeah, I was pretty sure I could make the shot, but I knew there was still a risk.

A risk I probably shouldn't have taken.

I knew with ninety-five percent certainty that I could make the shot. But what about the remaining five percent?

What if I had missed? And he had shot Aspen dead?

I can't even allow myself to go there.

"There's still so much I don't know," Aspen says with a sigh. "Like why the albino was impersonating Greg Wallace, why Greg was killed, why Harrison disowned Taylor..."

We pull up in front of the beach house. Luke drives into the garage and goes in the back way. Aspen and I go in the front door.

Jed and Edgar greet us with lots of jumping and licking.

That puts a smile on Aspen's face, so I'm forever grateful to those dogs.

When we are finally settled on the deck, and the dogs are playing, I turn to Luke.

Katelyn and Aspen are talking, and while I know I should let Aspen in on what's going on, and I will, right now she needs to be with Katelyn.

"What did you find out?"

"Just that Harrison was the bad guy, not his brother. He framed him."

Luke turns to me. "How did you figure it out?"

"It was a hunch, really. I just had a feeling when I walked in that office that something was off. Then I saw the South Pacific conch shell on his desk. The only time I've ever seen a shell like that was on Derek Wolfe's island. When I went to rescue"—I clear my throat—"Emily."

Luke simply nods.

He doesn't add anything, and I don't expect him to.

I shot him that day, in the shoulder. Nearly the exact same shot that he gave to Harrison Wallace today.

"Where'd you learn to shoot?" I ask Luke.

"My old man, of course. You saw the shooting range in his bunker."

I nod. "So not on the streets of LA? Hustling drugs?"

"I never hustled drugs on the street. I was higher up than that."

I say nothing.

He's probably waiting for me to acknowledge that he's not that man anymore. That he saved my life today. Man, I totally don't want to do that.

But damn...

He thanked me. He thanked me for what I did for Katelyn when we were both being held captive by King Winston.

Today he saved my life.

After I saved Aspen's.

Listen," I say, "I'm in your debt now."

Luke draws in a breath and then exhales. "No. We'll call it even."

I nod. "Thank you. I'm glad you were there to take Wallace out of commission before he shot me. Or worse yet, Aspen."

"That wouldn't have been pretty."

"I know. A left-handed shot. He could've done some damage."

"But he didn't. And he's going to be put away now."

"Is he? I just have a feeling that Chris Pollack and the albino are not long for this world."

"It doesn't matter. You and Aspen got the whole story out of him. You'll need to testify."

I nod. "So what's the connection to the albino?" I ask.

"Turns out he was a buddy of Wallace's from the island. He's the one who took care of Greg Wallace in prison. Seems Greg kept protesting, saying he was an innocent man, that he had been framed. The thing is? He never knew his brother was the one who framed him. No one believed him because he'd been dishonorably discharged from the Navy."

"Right. Darnell Davis told me all about that."

"Right," Luke says.

"So what happened then? Harrison must have used Greg's name when he went to the island."

"Yeah. Greg Wallace's name was on that manifest. Harrison used his brother's name to go to the island and commit horrific acts, and somehow or another he met the albino, Fernando Smith. Whether they knew each other in LA, I don't know. It doesn't really matter."

"How did Fernando Smith end up taking Greg Wallace's place in prison?"

"He got in under the guise of being a guard. Then he took care of Greg and simply put on his prison orange jumpsuit. Obviously they had a man on the inside helping. The guards don't pay a lot of attention to the prisoners. They're all numbers. Not faces or names."

"But Smith is albino. Surely they'd remember him."

"Nope. They see all kinds in prison, and they cease to be human to the guards after a while. Apparently Smith had a deal with Harrison to get sprung after Pollack was taken care of."

I nod. "It's a pretty brilliant plan when you think about it."

"I know. Somehow the albino escaped prosecution. The name of Fernando Smith doesn't appear anywhere on any of the manifests."

"Well, he was there. He..." I shake my head. "I wish I could kill that motherfucker with my bare hands."

"Yeah. Now you know how I feel about Chris Pollack."

I nod.

Seems Luke and I have finally found common ground.

I'm not sure I'll ever call him a friend.

But at least I can call him an ally.

I don't feel like he's my enemy anymore.

I believe he truly cares about Katelyn. I only wish he could've cared about my sister that same way, but then? Things may have turned out completely differently.

Sometimes things happen for a reason. Little puzzle pieces all fall into place, kind of like Tetris.

And maybe Luke is part of the puzzle that brought me to Aspen.

He did save my life today. And for that I can't help but be grateful.

"So..." I rake my fingers through my hair. "Help on the inside? How do we find out who's helping them? And how do we get our hands on this albino?"

"I've been thinking about that," Luke says.

"Yeah, so have I. There's only one way, isn't there? Aspen's going to have to file a report. Tell the police what the albino did to her."

Luke nods. "That's the only way. I mean, you and I both have contacts. The Wolfes have contacts. We can get them all offed, but I made a promise to myself when I asked Katelyn to marry me that I would be legit. I wouldn't commit any crimes or cause any crimes to be committed."

"You just shot a man today," I say.

"So did you, and that's different. I was defending someone."

I nod. "Yeah, so was I. Is this going to affect your immunity deal?"

"No. I've already talked to my old man about that. Technically, I'm not supposed to be carrying a firearm, but my old man cut a deal with the officer on my case."

"And you're okay with that?"

"I am. Because I saved your life today, Buck. Your life is important to Aspen and important to Katelyn. The two of them are important to me."

I nod.

That's what it all comes down to in the end.

He loves Katelyn, and I love Aspen.

I love Katelyn and he loves Aspen, as well.

The two of them are what bind us together.

We're no longer bound by my sister, but by the women we love.

And I can learn to live with that.

I have to.

46

ASPEN

I'm still shaking when I go to bed.

Buck comes to me, holds me.

He doesn't try to fuck me or even kiss me.

Instinctively, he knows what I need.

I could've died today.

Buck could've died today.

We're here. We're alive.

So why am I lying here like a dead fish?

I turn in his arms, and I press my lips to his.

"Baby?"

"Please. I need you. Make love to me. Slowly this time. Show me why we're still here. Show me what's important in life. What's beautiful."

He kisses me then, a sweet yet passionate kiss, and as soon as we're naked, I lift my leg over his hips, and he slides into me.

Such sweet completion.

And exactly what I need in this moment.

~

THE NEXT MORNING, a detective from the LAPD and an agent from the FBI come to the house to talk to me.

Katelyn sits, holding my hand, while Buck sits on my other side with his arm around me.

And I tell my story.

My memory—the one that wasn't very reliable when I first left the island and even after I got to Manhattan—now has no holes.

I tell the whole story.

All about the albino, and all the other men who hunted me, used me, tortured me, raped me. Violated me in the most horrific of ways.

Then the detective—a woman—takes me privately into one of the bedrooms.

I disrobe, and she takes photographs of my body.

I'm not embarrassed. I'm not humiliated.

It's freeing, in a way.

This is what it will take to get the albino put away for a long time.

For good.

As for Pollack?

Katelyn doesn't have to have her body photographed. First of all, he didn't put any marks on her. And secondly? We've already got him on two murders and an assault and battery.

But Katelyn has told her story anyway.

Buck hugs me and soothes me after the detective and the FBI agent leave.

"We're almost there, baby," he says, kissing the outer rim

of my ear. "Almost. Soon we'll be able to leave all of this behind us."

I hope he's right.

I'm almost afraid to let myself feel that he may be right.

The albino, as far as we know, is still in prison impersonating Greg Wallace.

Chris Pollack is in the county jail, awaiting his trial.

And Harrison Wallace?

He's in the hospital, his one good hand handcuffed to his bed.

Taylor is dead.

Gloria and her husband are dead.

Nancy is in prison for six months after pleading guilty.

I've succeeded, for the most part.

I succeeded in getting all of my questions answered.

So why do I feel so...

What exactly do I feel?

I'm loved, cherished by a wonderful man.

A man I love in return, who I know will be with me, by my side, for the rest of our lives.

I smile against his shoulder.

Still... something else isn't sitting right with me.

I have the most wonderful man in the world.

I have answers to my questions, and the people who sent me to that island have paid or will pay.

I have Luke and Katelyn, the best friends a girl could ask for.

I have my mother and my father, who love me.

And I have little Edgar.

I nuzzle into Buck's shoulder.

Whatever this thing is that's bugging me?

I will tamp it down.

Because my life is good now.

I don't want that to change.

And ruminating on something that may not even exist?

I don't need that.

Still… The albino's out there.

If he wasn't supposed to be in prison in the first place—if he only went there to take the place of Greg Wallace—he won't stay there for long, even with the testimony I just gave to the LAPD and the FBI. He clearly has connections, which is how he got in there in the first place. He can get out…

And he can come for me.

Harrison Wallace is no consequence at the moment. He's recovering from two gunshot wounds, and he's handcuffed to his hospital bed.

But he has people on the outside—people who got rid of his brother and put the albino in his place.

I still haven't gotten revenge on everyone who did me wrong.

I want them all to pay.

Especially the albino.

He needs to pay for what he's done to me. But how? As far as the authorities know, he's Greg Wallace. I'm still not exactly sure how all that took place.

The only one who can tell us is Harrison Wallace, and he's recuperating from gunshot wounds.

If only…

"Buck?"

"Yeah baby?"

"How do I know? How do I know the albino will pay for what he did to me?"

"Well, you just gave a statement to the local PD and the feds."

"But he's in prison as Greg Wallace."

"Baby, it's already been started. They're going to check the fingerprints against Greg Wallace's. They're on file because he was originally framed by his brother. They will easily be able to prove that the albino is not Greg Wallace."

I heave a sigh. And tears squirm out of my eyes.

I know all this. I don't know why I'm worried. The albino will get what's coming to him.

As for Greg Wallace?

In his way, he was as much a victim as I am.

Victimized by his own brother—framed for actions he did not commit. But also dishonorably discharged from the Navy.

"We have to tell my dad," I say. "He has to know that it wasn't Greg Wallace—the SEAL he got kicked out—who hurt me. He thinks this is his fault."

"You can call him whenever you're ready, baby."

I nod. "I will. When I'm thinking clearly."

"Aspen, no one can blame you if you're not thinking clearly. Believe me, I've been there."

I cup his stubbly cheek, run my thumb over his lower lip. He's so handsome, my Buck. So big and strong and magnificent.

And he's been through...

I don't even know everything that he's been through. Just like he doesn't know everything that I've been through. We have our lifetimes to learn everything about each other. And some of those things? Some of those things we may just keep bottled inside.

Luke and Katelyn are out on the deck with the dogs.

"You feel like a swim?" Buck asks.

"Not especially," I say.

"What then?" he asks. "What can I do for you?"

"All I need from you is your love, Buck." I brush my lips over his. "All I need is your love."

47

BUCK

One month later...

"On the first count, murder in the first degree, we, the jury, find the defendant, Christopher Pollack, guilty. On the second count, murder in the first degree, we find the defendant, Christopher Pollack, guilty. On the third count, assault and battery with the intent to kill, we find the defendant, Christopher Pollack, guilty."

Aspen relaxes next to me.

I can almost see the tension flowing off her in visible waves.

Katelyn, sitting on Aspen's other side, also relaxes. Pollack is the man who tormented her the most on that island.

And he will be going away for a long time.

Luke and I both pulled some strings through our contacts to make sure Pollack was safe during his time at the county jail while he awaited trial. We wanted the system to do its work for once.

And it did.

Now? What happens to Pollack once he gets to prison? Well...that's between him and his fellow inmates.

Fernando Smith, the albino and Aspen's worst tormentor, pleaded guilty to first degree rape, assault and battery, unlawful imprisonment, and a host of other crimes. Two weeks ago, he was killed by a fellow inmate.

He was violated with a knife, and he bled to death.

How did a fellow prisoner get a knife? Connections, though not any of ours.

That said, none of us shed any tears when we heard the news.

I expect the same thing to happen to Pollack once he gets to that same facility.

It's a funny thing about prisoners. They're all criminals, for the most part. But they really don't like people who abuse women and children. That makes you a pariah in prison, and the albino paid the price. No doubt Pollack will as well.

And if it happens, we won't mourn the loss.

Aspen and I have been going to therapy together for the last couple of weeks.

She did what she came to do. She found out the story behind her abduction.

And everyone involved in it is paying.

Harrison Wallace took his own life while he was still in the hospital, leaving a few mysteries unsolved. He swallowed enough fentanyl to kill several people. How did he get it?

No one knows.

And no one's asking any questions.

Once Aspen and Katelyn went public with their stories? Everyone pretty much felt he got what he deserved.

So yeah... Therapy.

Aspen and I both need to deal better with our PTSD, and we're getting there.

With each other, we're getting there.

Aspen's need for vengeance seems to be satisfied, and she's not interested in tracking down any of the other men from the island who hurt her.

Most of them are probably in prison or dead anyway. Or they've disappeared and will never return.

We leave the courtroom, and then we go home to our apartment. Aspen and I didn't want to stay in Luke's beach house forever, so we got our own place here.

Will we stay?

We're not sure yet, but we'll be here for another two weeks.

Tomorrow is Luke and Katelyn's wedding, and we'll be dog sitting for them while they're on their honeymoon.

We'll be staying at the beach house since Jed isn't used to an apartment.

Edgar will enjoy his company.

WE'RE AT A SMALL CHURCH.

Yes. The man formerly known as Lucifer Raven is getting married in a church.

But at this point in my life, I don't have any issue with that. Luke Ashton has finally made me see who he is now.

His brother, Sebastian Ashton, stands beside him in the front of the church. They both are clad in black tuxedos.

A string quartet begins Mozart's wedding march, and I look toward the back, where Aspen—my beautiful Aspen—begins walking toward the front in her bridesmaid's dress.

It's dark pink—and it clings to her. It's strapless, and yes, some of her scars are visible.

And they're beautiful.

Then comes Katelyn, flanked by her parents, James and Farrah Brooks.

Her dress is also strapless—and instead of white she chose ivory because of her fair skin.

And yes—some of her scars are also visible.

These two women are walking down the aisle as they are.

Pure beauty. I watch as the scene before me unfolds.

I watch as Katelyn hands her bouquet of roses to Aspen, and I watch as Luke's brother hands him the rings.

I watch these two people become husband and wife. I watch as they gaze into each other's eyes and repeat traditional vows.

Inside my breast pocket is my surprise for Aspen.

A diamond ring that once belonged to my great-grandmother.

Tonight, after the reception, I'm going to ask Aspen to be my wife.

Because together, we're stronger than we are apart.

We're the other halves of each other.

A sum that is more than its parts.

We are...one.

EPILOGUE

ASPEN

Three months later...

Buck and I get married at Luke and Katelyn's beach house.

I was surprised Buck agreed to it, but he and Luke seem to have finally come to an understanding between them.

Katelyn and I are ecstatic about it. Because we're besties, the four of us will be spending a lot of time together.

Katelyn is, of course, my maid of honor, and Buck's sister Emily is my bridesmaid. Coming back to this house couldn't have been easy for her, but she did it for Buck and for me.

Buck has two best men. His brother, Johnny, and his fellow SEAL, Leif Ramsey. Also known as Phoenix.

I'm dancing with Phoenix later. He's tall and muscular, like Buck, but there the similarities end. Leif is blond and blue-eyed with light skin.

"Thank you for being here," I tell him. "For Buck. It means everything to him."

"I'll always be here for Buck," Leif says. "We're brothers."

His phone buzzes.

"Do you mind?"

"Of course not."

He leads me off the dance floor and looks at his phone.

"Oh, shit."

"Is anything the matter?"

"I need to talk to Buck."

"Leif, this is our wedding day. Please..."

"I know, Aspen. And I'm sorry."

Buck is on the dance floor with his sister.

Emily and Luke seem to have made their peace as well, and for that I'm grateful. Emily is radiant—she looks like Buck in female form—and she seems ecstatic with her significant other, Scotty, a half-Hawaiian surfer boy who's now studying to be a licensed psychologist.

A moment later, Buck is leaving the dance floor with Leif. They go inside the house.

I wait.

And I wait.

Only a few minutes have passed, but I can't take it any longer. I head into the house to find them.

They're deep in conversation when—

"Aspen, baby."

"Exactly what's going on?"

"I'm so sorry," Buck says, "but I need to go back to New York."

"All right. In two weeks. After our trip to the Virgin Islands."

"I promise you, baby, we will have the honeymoon of the century. But we have to put it off for a little while."

The spoiled little girl inside me wants to stomp and hold my breath, but I don't. This is Buck. The man who loves me.

And he wouldn't make me postpone my honeymoon unless it was very important.

He is who he is. He's Buck. He saves people. He wouldn't be the man I love if he didn't do that.

"Why? What is it?"

"It's another one of the women from the island." Buck shakes his head. "Opal. She's in trouble."

I swallow. "Kelly?"

Kelly was different. She used to get jealous when someone was chosen over her. None of us understood her. Of course, none of us tried to understand anything while we were there. We were simply trying to keep our own heads above water.

"Yeah," Phoenix says. "A threat has been made against her...by another woman from the island."

LEIF AND KELLY'S story begins in *Opal*, coming soon!

PLUS, read about Carly Vance—Jade from the island—in *Scarred*, book one in The Billion Heirs, my upcoming series with *USA Today* bestselling author Vanessa Vale! Available October 11, 2022.

He's inherited billions, but he must leave his home and family to claim it.

She's no longer a captive, yet will she ever be free?

Austin Bridger is struggling to keep his seaplane business afloat and help his ailing mother. When his father, who never acknowledged his existence, dies, he leaves his billions to Austin and his two half brothers. The catch? To receive the inheritance, they must all live on his father's Montana ranch for a year. To Austin, the money's tainted, but because he desperately needs every dime, he has no choice but to leave Seattle.

Carly Vance was a student in veterinary school when her dream was shattered. Abducted from a diner in her small town, she was held captive on a South Pacific island for three years. Now she's home, but her scars run deep. Trying to reclaim her life, she bravely takes a job in Bridger Ranch's stables.

Sparks fly when Carly crosses paths with Austin, but they both hold secrets—secrets that could keep them apart forever.

EXCERPT FROM SCARRED

AUSTIN

"Who'd you piss off?"

I glance up at Ed, the dock guy helping me to load the coolers of fresh oysters into the cargo area of the plane. My back is to the shore and I don't dare turn around. Not yet.

Ed looks down the length of the dock to someone I assume is heading our way. It's probably Cara—or Tara—from Saturday. After our night together, she somehow found out about my business—because we didn't do much talking—and has been calling around the clock. Showing up takes stalker to a new level because I am always straight with a woman. One night. No strings. All the orgasms she can take.

"Fuck," I say under my breath and take a second to close my eyes. Just what I need. Baggage besides the seafood I am about to shuttle to the resort up in the San Juans. "Redhead? Legs for miles?" I ask.

Ed's bushy eyebrows head north. "I wish. How about male, fifty and balding. I'd peg him as IRS except the guy's wearing a bolo tie."

I turn on the worn dock, the water lapping at the side. I catch a whiff of the briny tang of the outgoing tide. The man, who does appear to be in his fifties, is headed our way and he's definitely not Cara. Or Tara. Ed's guess is pretty good, but as far as I know, the tax man is the one guy who doesn't have an issue with me.

"Mr. Bridger!" The man raises his hand as if to hail a cab. He does have on a string tie along with a white shirt and crisp jeans. And he holds a square leather briefcase. Definitely a creditor.

Just what I need. I have enough issues dealing with the healthcare system and my mother's bills on the phone. In person is a whole new level of pressure I don't want.

I set my hands on my hips and prepare for a battle. "If you want money, it'll only happen if I get these oysters in the air. They're not the paying customers you probably want to see, but they are alive. For now."

He stops in front of me and wipes his brow. For the Northwest, the weather is warm. Almost hot. Another reason to get the plane in the air instead of lingering. Oysters and heat aren't a good combo.

He glances at the plane and then back to me. "I'm not here to take money from you, Mr. Bridger. I'm Tom Shankle, lawyer from Shankle, Smith, and Brazee."

Great. A lawyer. "I'm being sued." I turn my back on him, grab another cooler, and pass it to Ed. "Even better."

"You're not being sued," Shankle assures me.

With a quick glance, I see him smile.

"You make visits to everyone who owes you money?" I stop mid-reach and stand upright. At six-two, I have five inches or more on the man. "If you bothered my mother with your money-grubbing shit—"

He holds up a hand. "I assure you I didn't bother her. She's not the reason for this visit. I hope her current treatments for multiple sclerosis are going well."

I frown. What's his angle?

"You know a lot about the health of a woman who's not the reason for your visit."

Mom's latest meds are part of a trial and aren't covered by insurance. Expensive. But working. She currently only has mild symptoms and I want it to stay that way, although she can no longer pilot trips for the business she founded. Shankle pulling the plug on the treatment was a no-fucking-go.

Shankle rubs his jawline. "I've kept tabs on you."

Ed loads the last cooler and shuts the cargo door with a hearty slam that shakes the plane. He nods and ducks around the two of us as best he can for a guy of his size. I can't blame him for steering clear of my shit, whatever the hell it is. Going to the back rope line, he waits for me to climb in and do my pre-flight checks. That's right, time to go. He'll help other planes that use this dock.

"Why the hell would you do that?" I growl, not liking anyone to *keep tabs on me*. Especially a lawyer.

"I've tried to reach you for the past three weeks." Shankle follows me to the front of the plane.

"Sorry, been busy running a business here. But you know that since you're keeping those tabs and all." I climb onto the runner and reach to open the door, ready to get the hell out of here.

"I represent your father. Jonathan Bridger."

I freeze for a second and then turn, bobbing up and down along with the plane on the water.

"I'm not sure which is worse. Creditors or my fucking

sperm donor," I grumble and glare. "Or a lawyer representing him."

"I assure you, I bear good news," Shankle replies with a shaky smile.

"I don't give a shit about the man just as he's never given one about me. Good news? The only thing you can tell me that I'd consider positive is that he's dead."

He huffs out a laugh. "It seems that I may have made your day then. He is, in fact, dead."

I blink, processing what he just said. "Holy shit." Then I grin.

The fucker married my mother and then divorced her before I was even born. Left her with nothing. Sure, required child support, but that wasn't what she wanted from him. She expected love from a spouse. Not to be abandoned and for him to move on to another woman. Or two. Or fucking more.

My father was never a part of my life. Hell, I never even met him. Just hated his guts for what he did to my mom.

"How?" Yeah, I want to know what finally brought the man down.

"Aneurysm."

So instant and without any pain. Too bad.

"Thanks for letting me know." I open the cockpit door, ready to climb in and leave the bastard behind, just like always.

"There's more," Shankle adds.

I glance up at the sky. "That's enough for me. He's dead. Thanks for letting me know."

"I need fifteen minutes of your time."

"So do those oysters in the back." I point to the rear of the plane.

"Fine. I'll ride with you."

I glare again. Not what I expected. He steps down onto the runner behind me and opens the rear door, the one for passengers. The plane bobs from the shift in weight.

Lovering Seaplane usually takes passengers, but for supplemental income, we run supplies and various cargo. Like oysters. I'm used to customers, but not ones who climb aboard last minute for a chat. In Shankle's case, it's to talk to me and most likely piss me off. Especially if it has to do with my father.

He can go along for the ride, but I don't have to make it easy on him.

I hold the door open as graciously as I possibly can. He tosses in his briefcase and awkwardly climbs up and into the back seat.

"Ever flown in a seaplane before?" I ask casually.

"Nothing smaller than the commuter jet from Missoula," he replies.

I smirk and glance at Ed, who shrugs. I climb into the pilot's seat and begin my pre-flight checklist.

"Mr. Bridger. Jonathan Bridger had a sizeable estate in Montana and—"

I hold up a hand to stop him. "I need to complete my checks, Shankle. In silence, unless you want me to miss something and risk us taking a two thousand-foot-swan dive into the Sound."

Shankle remains silent as I strap in and work through the list I have memorized, getting the engines on. I give Ed a thumbs up, and we're untied and in the air quickly, headed north. I adjust the yoke as we're buffeted by the high-level winds. Nothing too strong, but I don't fight them.

"As I was saying," Shankle shouts over the noise of the engines.

Out of the corner of my eye I can see him trying to get his balance. I can barely hear him with my headset on so I tap my ear and glance back at him.

He grabs the headset in the back for passengers and puts it on. "Can you hear me now?"

His voice comes through all too clearly, annoying me, so I tip the yoke, dipping the right wing. The plane plunges a hundred feet or so and I pull up. When the guy has to reach out to keep from flying across the cabin, I can't help a slight smile.

"Might want to strap in," I say. "Could get bumpy up here with choppy air and all."

It isn't all that rough. Low wind, clear visibility. A little bit of chop, just like the water below, but doable, if you're not prone to motion sickness.

His seatbelt clinks. "You have two half brothers."

My smile slips. I know about them. Both younger and from the women who took my mom's place. I turn the yoke again, dropping the right wing once more. Shankle gasps.

"The three of us aren't going to make a fort in the backyard and take blood oaths, Shankle. Get to the point."

I tap my sunglasses up my nose and straighten the plane. There is no autopilot so I keep my gaze on the horizon and the tree-covered rolling hills of the Pacific Northwest.

"You and your brothers are heirs to his estate."

The man—our father—was rich. Obscenely so, and since I turned eighteen, I haven't seen a dime of it. Before then, I didn't get much. Enough for clothes and extra food. He moved on and so did my mom. She started the seaplane company from the ground—or in her case, the Puget Sound—up.

"Great. Mail the china and stamp collection to the

company address. You didn't need to come all the way to Seattle." I don't raise my voice. I don't have to. I'm sure he can tell how much I hate my father through the headset loud and clear.

His laugh comes through just as clearly. "I assure you, Mr. Bridger, you received more than a stamp collection. That's why I've been trying to reach you. Jonathan Bridger's fortune is estimated at over three billion dollars. You, along with your half brothers, Miles and Chance, are the sole inheritors."

The plane takes a nosedive. I'm not fucking with Shankle this time. I just can't believe what I'm hearing. The engine noise changes and my seat rattles.

"I'm a...what? A fucking billionaire?" I ask, righting the plane.

We're now a few hundred feet lower and Shankle's stomach is probably in his throat. Mine is too, for a completely different reason.

Money like that means no more oyster runs to ensure Mom's medicine is paid for this month. Mom can go to that specialist we read up on in Chile. Hell, she can *buy* Chile. No more creditors or business problems because she's sick. It means a second... or even a third seaplane. The charter business she started thirty years ago won't fold.

I pull back on the yoke and aim for the stars. I can't help the grin and a whoop of happiness. Dear old Dad can rot in hell while Mom gets well and flies again.

"I'll give you my bank account information when we land. You're right, Shankle. You do have good news." I strum the yoke with my fingers, feeling fucking great for the first time in months.

Shankle is quiet, and I glance over my shoulder at him.

He has his briefcase in his lap and a small stack of papers in his hands. "There is a catch."

I glance out the front window again and adjust course slightly. I've flown the area enough to recognize the sea and land below. Which island is which. There's no radar. No complex instrumentation.

"A catch," I echo. Of course there is.

"You must return to Bridger Ranch in Montana."

Hmm. A few days away may impact flights. But if I have a billion dollars, what does it matter?

"I can swing a week off."

"You'll need a little more than a week." Shankle clears his throat. "The will clearly stipulates that all three Bridger sons must live at Bridger Ranch for the duration of one year to receive a dime."

"What the fuck?" I shout. "A year? I can't live in Montana for a year. As you're aware, my mother is sick and on special trial drugs. If I don't get the money for a year, I can't stop working. The company will go under, and Mom—"

"It was your father's last wish."

"That I live in bumfuck Montana for a year? Give up my life, my business, risk my mother's health all because some asshole is making me jump through hoops?"

As punishment, I dip the plane again, feel the pull against my harness.

Shankle whimpers.

A father who I never met and is dead—*dead*—is fucking with me and will continue to do so for an entire year. I have to go to Montana to get the money that will help my mother and save the company. But going will most likely make my mother's symptoms worse and will definitely hurt the business since I won't be able to fly.

"If it makes you feel any better, your brothers—"

"*Half* brothers."

"—aren't any happier. However, I *was* on land when I shared the news with them."

The cove where I will land appears in the distance. I adjust the flaps to begin our descent.

"We'll be on the ground soon, Shankle."

Really soon since I decide to come in hot. If I'm headed to Montana, I might as well have a little fun before I'm grounded. And landlocked. And stuck with two men who share tainted blood.

"We're the billion heirs," I mutter.

Only a deadbeat—and *dead*—father would ruin it all.

A NOTE FROM HELEN

Dear Reader,

Thank you for reading *Buck*. If you want to find out about my current backlist and future releases, please visit my website, like my Facebook page, and join my mailing list. If you're a fan, please join my Facebook street team (Hardt & Soul) to help spread the word about my books. I regularly do awesome giveaways for my street team members.

If you enjoyed the story, please take the time to leave a review. I welcome all feedback.

I wish you all the best!

Helen

Sign up for my newsletter here:

http://www.helenhardt.com/signup

ACKNOWLEDGMENTS

Thank you so much to the following individuals who helped make this story shine: My editor (and son!), Eric McConnell, my cover artist, Kim Killion, and my awesome beta readers, Karen Aguilera, Serena Drummond, Linda Pantlin Dunn, and Angela Tyler. You all rock!

ABOUT THE AUTHOR

#1 *New York Times*, #1 *USA Today*, and #1 *Wall Street Journal* bestselling author Helen Hardt's passion for the written word began with the books her mother read to her at bedtime. She wrote her first story at age six and hasn't stopped since. In addition to being an award-winning author of romantic fiction, she's a mother, an attorney, a black belt in Taekwondo, a grammar geek, an appreciator of fine red wine, and a lover of Ben and Jerry's ice cream. She writes from her home in Colorado, where she lives with her family. Helen loves to hear from readers.

Please sign up for her newsletter here:
http://www.helenhardt.com/signup
Visit her here:
http://www.helenhardt.com

CPSIA information can be obtained
at www.ICGtesting.com
Printed in the USA
LVHW041938140822
725927LV00002B/157

9 781952 841132